'Butch whacked his stick against the rails of the allotments fence and then walked towards the path that led down to the Old Line. "Two of you come wi' me, the rest stand guard."

But Butch never even started down the path because they heard the sound of something coming up from the darkness towards him. The sound of something heavy, scattering stones as it ran, something breathing heavily as it climbed.

Butch was frozen into stillness. They all were.

Then Elvis shot into view.

"It's back down there!" he shouted. "That Ghost Dog! It's real big!" At first they didn't believe him. Butch even took a step forward to capture him, but then they all saw something large and grey coming out of the mist towards them, and they all heard a low, long growl.

And they all ran then.'

The news that a huge ghostly dog is on the prowl shocks the neighbourhood. No one can talk of anything else, and Billy is sure that the monstrous hound lies in wait for him round every corner. But then comes the terrifying, and completely unexpected, encounter . . .

Dick Cate is an award-winning author who has written many books for children. GHOST DOG is the first title in his lively and amusing series about Billy Robinson, his family and friends. Its sequels, TWISTERS and FOXCOVER, will also be available in Yearling Books.

GHOST DOG
DICK CATE

**ILLUSTRATED BY
CAROLINE BINCH**

YEARLING BOOKS

GHOST DOG

A YEARLING BOOK 0 440 862116

Originally published in Great Britain by Victor Gollancz Ltd.

PRINTING HISTORY
Victor Gollancz edition published 1987
Yearling edition published 1989

This book is set in 14/16 pt Century Schoolbook

Yearling Books are published by Transworld Publishers Ltd.,
61–63 Uxbridge Road, Ealing, London W5 5SA, in Australia by
Transworld Publishers (Australia) Pty. Ltd., 15–23 Helles
Avenue, Moorebank, NSW 2170, and in New Zealand by
Transworld Publishers (N.Z.) Ltd., Cnr. Moselle and Waipareira
Avenues, Henderson, Auckland.

Printed and bound in Great Britain by
Cox & Wyman Ltd., Reading, Berks.

Billy

Chapter 1

The first time Billy heard about the Ghost Dog, it was made out to be a joke.

They mentioned it at the end of the local news programme on the telly, where they usually told you about somebody's goldfish that had drowned, or a cat that could sing *God Save the Queen* upside down and accompany itself on the banjo at the same time.

'Now it may not exactly be Hallowe'en, viewers,' the announcer was saying, 'but some of you may be still interested in ghouls and ghosties!'

Everybody called him Lord La-de-dah because he had such a posh voice.

'Those of you interested in ghosts will certainly enjoy the *spirit* of our last news item tonight!'

He was always cracking corny jokes.

But Billy was interested in ghosts, if only because they had one in the family. According to his grandma, Billy's grandad had been doing duty as a ghost for several years now. Mind you, if you believed what Billy's grandma told you, you'd believe anything, because she was the biggest liar on this earth. She even cheated at cards.

'This story comes from Bowburn, in the very centre of our fabulous region,' Lord La-de-dah continued, 'and concerns a dog, a rather special dog.'

He peered at them through his thick goggles and smiled.

'I wish he'd get on with it!' said Billy's dad.

'Over-busy showing off his teeth!' said Billy's mam.

'Now I suppose that up here in the Frozen North we are quite famous for breeding dogs. Indeed, you might say wearing flat hats, and breeding good dogs are about the only things we are famous for!'

'Far too big for his boots!' said Billy's mam.

'He wants tekkin' down a peg or two!' said Billy's dad.

They both hated him like poison. Everybody did. Elvis Potter called him Sir Hugely Goboil.

'But this dog is different, actually,' he said. 'It's a Ghost Dog! Yes – and we kid you good Northern Folk not – a dog of the ghostly variety has been seen mooching about on the perimeters of Bowburn Colliery and terrorizing the local natives!'

'How dare the man call them that?' asked Billy's mam. 'Anybody'd think Bowburn was in the middle of the jungle!'

'The man's not altogether right in the head, man, Alice,' said Billy's dad. 'By rights he ought to be under a doctor.'

'We have been given to understand that no less than five good people of Bowburn have actually clapped their eyes on this strange creature, though – perhaps not surprisingly – not one of them has actually managed to come to grips with it!'

'It ought to come to grips with you, mister,' said Billy's mam, 'and right sharp!'

'A good bite in the backside might do him a power of good!' said Billy's dad.

'Now this Ghost Dog is very elusive, viewers. Very, very, elusive. It comes out of the mists – or is it out of the Broon Ale?'

'I knew, sure as shot, he'd mention booze before the night was out,' said Billy's mam.

'The man's obsessed with it, Alice.'

'And a certain Mr Milburn in that celebrated region of our Beloved Northlands has managed to take a pot shot at it – though unfortunately to no avail . . .'

'Should've tekken a pot shot at you instead, mister!'

'Might've put him out of his misery!'

'Rather an unsporting gesture, that, I think – shooting at a Ghost Dog with a double-barrelled shotgun. Actually, I always thought we were rather fond of dumb animals up here in the Frozen North – for some obscure reason!'

'What's he mean by saying "we"?' asked Billy's mam. 'He's surely to goodness not classifying himself as one of us?'

'There's nowt I wouldn't put past that fellar, Alice.'

'Perhaps Mr Milburn might have done a little better if he had used a *silver* bullet!' Lord La-de-dah paused long enough for this witty remark to sink into the thick bonces of his viewers. Though, as far as Billy was concerned, what he had said only showed his own ignorance: a shotgun didn't fire bullets. 'You *did* remember to use a *silver* bullet, Mr Milburn?'

'Should've used a silver bullet on you,mister.'

'Two,' said Billy's dad. 'Or three.'

'They only use silver bullets on zombies, Dad,' said Billy.

'He knew that because he had seen a film about zombies round at Elvis Potter's house. He had seen it nineteen times. Mr Potter had made about fifty copies of it on his video machine.

'Don't interrupt when the telly's on, son,' said his dad.

'Anyhow, it's almost time we closed now, actually. But if you do just happen to see an enormous dog – grey, with luminous eyes – coming towards you out of the mists as you wend your way back from the chip-hole or the Broon Ale shop—'

'There we go again!'

'Obsessed!'

'—I wouldn't bother to shout for help. If I were you, actually, I'd just RUN!'

'I wish *you* would run, mister!'

'Aye! All the way to the North Pole! And never come back!'

'You couldn't run all the way to the North Pole, Dad,' said Billy. 'Your feet would sink through the water.'

'I wish you'd give over interrupting, Our Billy,' said his mam. 'You can see your dad's trying to concentrate.'

That'll be a job, and all, thought Billy, but he didn't say anything. The only thing his dad really

10

concentrated on was the sport, especially football. Not that Billy minded.

'As for me – and my colleague here in the studio, Valerie – I think we may very well be going home by taxi tonight, actually, eh, Val? All the way!' He leaned forward and gave all the poor halfwits outside the studio a nudge and a wink, just in case they didn't get it. The camera showed poor Valerie Whateverernamewas looking across at him and fingering her sharpened pencil like a mad murderess.

'If looks could kill, eh, Dick?'

'No love lost between them two!'

La-de-dah scooped his papers together and once more exhibited his false gnashers.

'Anyhow, thank you once more for looking in to *Looking Out* – and see you tomorrow night!'

'Not on your nelly!' said Billy's mam.

'We always watch it, Mam,' Billy reminded her. 'We never miss.'

'I'll not miss your lughole, young man!' said his dad. 'You'll get a clip round it in a minute if you don't watch out!'

Billy watched till the adverts ended and then he retreated into the kitchen, shutting the door behind him to blot out the noise of the telly, and started to construct himself a Doorstep Special.

Elvis Potter had told him the recipe. You got two thick slices of bread, plastered them with butter, then sprinkled sugar on the butter, then added jam, Bovril, and peanut butter to taste. It was delicious. The Potters were very fond of sandwiches: sandwiches were all they ever ate

11

unless the chip shop was open. Mr Potter always called sandwiches a square meal.

Billy was just starting on the demolition stage when he remembered the letter that had arrived that morning. He glanced up at the mantelpiece. It was still there. Almost hidden behind the teacaddy, exactly where his mother had put it at breakfast time.

Or almost exactly.

Chapter 2

Billy had known straight off where it had come from. He hadn't been watching all the Sherlock Holmes films on telly for nothing. He had recognized the scrawly handwriting straight off.

Anybody would have thought it had been written by a spider that had fallen into a barrel of Guinness and stopped the night there. But, in fact, it wasn't written by an inebriated spider. It was written by his sister, Sandra, who last Christmas had fallen off the end of the sofa after one glass of sherry and had to be picked up off the floor in a giggling fit.

Nothing unusual about his sister writing them a letter, of course. Nothing unusual at all. Ever since she'd shifted down to Barnsley – with her husband, Steven, and the baby – she had written to them every week, as near as makes no odds: mostly boring details about wallpaper and the price of disposable nappies.

What was unusual was the look on his mam's face as she read the letter. Usually she looked like a satisfied Buddha when she had a letter from Their Sandra in her hand. But this time a shadow had flitted over her face, she'd bit her lip and drawn in a sharp breath.

And then – even more unusual – instead of reading aloud all the best bits to Billy, she had folded the letter up, put it back in its envelope and then put the envelope behind the teacaddy where it was now.

Well, not exactly where it was now.

Billy noticed it was sticking out just a bit more than it had been. He guessed that the letter had probably been looked at again. Most likely when his dad got home from the factory, while Billy was still up at the allotment seeing to the hens and pigeons, which he did every night for his pocket money.

It was while he was pondering on this point that Billy noticed something else. His sharp ears told him that his mam and dad were whispering about something. He distinctly heard his mam say, 'What do you think we should do, Dick?' and his dad say, 'Shush, woman!' Then the telly was turned up.

They really were pathetic! Did they really think anybody wouldn't notice a thing like that?

Billy looked round the kitchen. He was searching for a glass. Recently he had read a book from the school library called *Tricks of Detection*, in which there was a chapter entitled The Well-Trained Ear – which made him think of a largish lughole, about the size of a bulldog, four legs, tail, and everything, trotting along obediently at somebody's heels and waiting to be told to 'SIT!'

But the chapter hadn't been anywhere as interesting as that. It was largely about keeping your ears pinned back in the doctor's waiting room in case somebody starting discussing how they were going to rob the local bank; or sticking a glass against a wall so you could overhear what people were saying in the next room.

But, naturally, there wasn't a glass in sight when he wanted one. They would all be in his mam's display cabinet in the other room. Billy had noticed that was often the way with invaluable tips that you read about in books.

He tried straining his ears. But it was no good. All he could hear was the telly. So he decided to go into the other room where he could hear more clearly.

'Whatever's that in your hand, Our Billy?' asked his mother as he went in.

She was putting on her topcoat and scarf, which she'd just got from the lobby by the front door.

Billy looked down at the sandwich.

'A sarni, Mam.'

'I've told you not to use that word, Billy. It looks more like a monstrosity if you ask me!'

'It'll be that silly Potter lad that's put him up to that,' said Billy's dad. He went into the kitchen, and came back with his cap on and Dot's lead in his hand.

'Where you going, Dad?'

'Just out for a walk, son. Your mother fancies a breath of fresh air.' He called Dot to him and fastened her lead on. 'We'll not be five minutes.'

'And I don't want any crumbs dropping on this carpet while I'm out,' his mam said. She picked up her purse from the sideboard. 'You can either get a plate or eat that thing out there. Suit yourself. And turn that television down if

16

you're going to watch it, Our Billy. We'll have the neighbours round before we know where we are.'

After they'd gone out of the front door Billy

twiddled the knobs on the telly for a bit, but there was nothing on so he switched it off.

He wondered why his mam had taken her purse. You didn't have to pay for breaths of fresh air nowadays, did you?

And when he went back into the kitchen to eat his Doorstep in there – because his mam would see the smallest crumb on the carpet the minute she came back – he noticed another funny thing.

The letter from Sandra had gone: his dad must have picked it up when he went in for his cap and the lead.

And putting the two funny things together – the purse and the letter – Billy felt he had a good idea what his mam and dad were up to.

He smiled to himself as he finally demolished his Doorstep. Then he sided the things away and made sure the fire was all right.

He left the kitchen light on so he wouldn't have to grope his way across the yard. There was a chill in the air as he went up the back street, and the mist was thickening.

It *did* seem a funny night for a breath of fresh air.

Chapter 3

It was nice and snug in the Potters' house, though.

Billy and Elvis were playing with the ferrets on the kitchen table. Elvis called them Pinky and Perky, and their cage was kept on top of the kitchen cupboard – where it was nice and handy.

That was another thing about the Potters' house: everything was kept handy. Like the hens which had their run under the table where Billy and Elvis were now sitting. They were fenced in with wire-netting, and there was a hole bored in the middle of the table so that after a meal you could just shove the crumbs down and that and give them their tea. It was all so convenient.

It was a bit smelly, mind you, but it saved you the bother of going out on a parky night to feed them. Mr Potter was very keen on labour-saving devices.

At the moment Mr Potter was in the other room making a copy of a video he had hired from the library. That was, more or less, how he made a living. He sold the copies cheap to people who couldn't afford to buy them in the shops. He was doing them a favour he said.

This video was about a little innocent-looking kid who was, in fact, the Devil come back to life.

He only had to look at a dog and it went howling down the street with its tail between its legs.

Billy wouldn't have minded being able to do that himself. There were a few dogs round the streets that he would liked to have sent howling down the street. Especially Mr Harle's big lurcher that always showed its teeth when he passed it. Only last week it had taken the seat out of Little Chuff's pants. Emma Ward had to rescue him by throwing a dustbin lid at it. Even then it had nearly attacked her as well. It was a mad thing.

A minute ago, when they'd been in the other room watching Elvis's big sister put safety pins through her ears, this kid on the video had looked real hard at a chap, and the next thing you knew this chap had chucked himself off a cliff right at this place where some monster sharks were cruising around looking for a bite to eat.

The funny thing was, this kid looked as if butter wouldn't melt in his mouth: really innocent. As a matter of fact, he reminded Billy of somebody, somebody he knew, but he couldn't remember who.

Just as Elvis was stuffing Perky down his shirt, his sister came into the kitchen all dolled-up for the disco.

'Poo!' said Elvis, because she had a load of scent on.

'Like me earrings, Our Kid?'

She'd hung little swastikas on her safety pins now.

'Smashing, Our Soss.'

Everybody called her Soss, though her real name was Marilyn. Billy had always thought it was because her face was like a sausage.

She went to the mirror and began to daub black lipstick on. Her hair stuck up, like a terrified porcupine's, and this week was dyed red, white and blue. Her long-term ambition was to have it shaved off.

Her mam and dad didn't mind. They thought it might suit her features. If Billy had suggested to his mother having his hair shaved off, she would have thrown a blue fit and all her hair would have dropped out. But Mr and Mrs Potter were liberal-minded in that respect. Elvis and Soss didn't know how lucky they were. It was only Soss's boyfriend who objected to the haircut; he said he didn't fancy kissing a skinhead.

'I'm off,' she said as she went out of their back door.

'You can say that again!' said Elvis. 'Twice.'

'That again!' Soss said, laughing at him.

They heard her clopping across the yard in her wedgies and then nearly shutting their backyard gate (you couldn't properly shut their backyard gate because one of the hinges was hanging off and Mr Potter was always too busy doing other things to mend it).

'Cliff's getting a war party up on Saturday,' said Elvis. Perky poked his head out of the top of Elvis's shirt and nibbled his ear. Elvis giggled. 'He's gettin' passionate about us!'

'What war party?'

'To raid the Crag Enders.'

Cliffy Butcher was always getting up war parties to raid the Crag Enders; he did it about every three weeks. When Mrs Drury, their teacher, was explaining how volcanoes needed to go off every so often, Billy had been reminded how Butch needed to bash somebody up every ten minutes or so and lead a full-scale war against the Crag Enders every three weeks.

'What for?' asked Billy.

'To get their Tarzan Swing.'

The Tarzan Swing was what the Crag Enders called a tatty bit of rope that dangled down from an oak tree in Doggy Wood. It must have hung there for donkey's years, because it was all white and frayed and worn away and nobody in their right senses would have pinched it.

In any case, in Butch's gang they had enough rope of their own to start with, yards and yards of it. They kept it in their den in the abandoned tunnel in the limestone quarry. Elvis's uncle had given them it. His name was Dasher and he drove a lorry that things were always falling off the back of.

'What do we want with an old tatty bit of rope?'

'It'll be great, man, Billy,' said Elvis, screwing up his face because Perky was getting even more passionate now.

'We'll be—ow—able to—yow—burn it up— ow—yow—or—ow—summat like—ow—that— yow!' He stood up and Perky was dangling down from his ear, his teeth firmly entrenched in the

lobe now, though, strangely enough, it seemed to lessen the yows from Elvis. 'An' we'll mebbies smash their camp up an' all, man—ow—it'll be—ow—great.'

To Billy it didn't seem all that great. It seemed daft. Fancy going down Doggy Wood to burn a tatty bit of rope when all the time you could be playing footer down at the rec!

It didn't seem sensible. But Billy didn't say anything to Elvis, because Elvis wasn't really the sort to be interested in anything sensible.

If he had been, he wouldn't have let ferrets dangle from his ears. And last week he wouldn't have let the rest of them all put him in a tippler truck on the top of the sand quarry, and push him down the incline until the truck hit the tripper and he was flung out over the edge to fall thirty feet onto the sandpile below.

Anybody else would have leapt out long before the tippler reached the end of the tracks: but Elvis had just lain there with his arms folded across his chest and his plastic Dracula teeth in, looking as contented as the Count himself after a good night out.

Mrs Potter screamed with delight when she came in with their fish and chips and saw the ferret still dangling from Elvis's ear.

'You really are daft, Our Elvis,' she said. She put the fish and chips down on the table. 'Just seen your mam and dad in the telephone,' she said to Billy. 'Your Sandra all right down in Barnsley, is she? She isn't in any sort of trouble?'

24

Chapter 4

The next morning, Wednesday, was when all the carry-on with Butch started.

Half a dozen of them were having a kickabout in the schoolyard before the bell went to call them in: Elvis, Billy, Joey, Bozzy, Daz, and Emma Ward.

If ever Billy had been forced into having another sister he would have chosen somebody like Emma Ward, because she was as near-perfect as a girl could ever be.

She wasn't like the other girls at all. For one thing, if you told Emma Ward a joke she actually got it. She used to burst out laughing when you got to the end. Not like most other girls: most other girls kept staring at you, as if you hadn't finished. Billy had once told Hazel Wittering (who everybody called Nuts) a joke nine times, an easy-peasy one, and she *still* hadn't got it.

Neither was Emma a teachers' pet – not like Samantha Soskiss, whose right hand spent most of its life fluttering about the top of her arm trying to catch Mrs Drury's attention. Samantha Soskiss was the sort who would have sold atomic secrets to the Russians for the promise of a gold star.

Nor did Emma Ward pong of scent. She was always neat and tidy – she washed her neck and that – but she didn't pong, not like most girls. Billy's sister used to pong like anything when she was first going out with Steven. Dot used to get the sneezles and the cat they had then used to belt outside, even when it was bucketing down, and wouldn't come back in till the smell had gone.

But what made Emma *really* outstanding as a girl was the fact that she was an ace footballer. And, as if to remind him of this point, she now intercepted one of his passes to Elvis, steered the ball neatly past Daz, then scored with a low, hard shot.

Bozzy missed completely and fell over with a clatter.

They'd only put him in goal because he had broken his leg and was on crutches. It seemed fairer that way. Up to now, he'd been doing all right by balancing on his two crutches and clearing the ball with a swing of his one good leg. But Bozzy was what you might call accident-prone: he'd even broken his leg playing Monopoly.

Emma and Billy were just helping him up and stuffing the crutches back under his arms so they could get on with the game, when they heard a yippee behind them and turning round they saw Butch riding on some poor mutt's back.

That was the trouble with Butch. He kept going through these phases. At the moment he was in a phase about wanting to own a horse. His dad couldn't afford a horse, so Butch rode

Emma

on little kids instead. It was understandable.

He rode to school on the backs of kids, and all the way back home again. Down at the rec, he went from the swings to the teacup and from the teacup to the slide without his feet ever touching the ground.

In the phase before this one he had fancied being a werewolf. This was after seeing a video at Elvis's called *The Mad Werewolf from Mars*. For a fortnight you couldn't walk up Bertha backs without Butch barking and leaping out at you from the dark, looking nine-parts barmy.

He really got into the part. He learnt to froth at the mouth really properly. The worst part was when all this gunge dripped onto his shirt. For a fortnight everybody had to call him Wolf. Then he got sick of it himself.

Trouble was, Butch wasn't the sort you could walk up to and tell him straight out he was nutty: if you did, he would just assume you fancied hospital food for a fortnight and give you one in the mush.

And it was no good fighting back, because hitting Butch was a bit like punching a brick wall. In fact, there were a few brick walls round where Billy lived which weren't anywhere as hard as Butch. Hitting him did your knuckles no good at all. There should have been a Government Health Warning on him, something like: HITTING THIS BOY COULD SERIOUSLY DAMAGE YOUR HEALTH.

Daz took one of his special shots: the ball went nineteen miles too high and over the wall into the field where nobody was supposed to go.

'Shall I get it for you?'

It was Little Chuff. He had just wandered over to watch them. He was clutching his Amazing Spiderman bag that his mam had just got him from a jumble sale.

'No thanks, Chuffy,' said Elvis. The trouble with Little Chuff was that if you let him go over into the field he would probably get lost in it. Elvis glanced round to make sure no teachers were snooping about, then went over the wall himself.

The funny thing was, there didn't seem to be a teacher in sight at all. They hadn't seen one all the time they'd been in the yard. Even funnier was the fact that Wednesday was Mr Fixby's duty day, and when Mr Fixby was in the yard you couldn't avoid seeing him, even if you wanted to, which you probably did.

Mr Fixby wasn't the most popular character in the world. He had hard blue eyes and a jaw like a steam-shovel. He was always boasting to his class about how many pints of beer he could drink in a night, and his belly hung two yards over his belt to prove it. He was also head-over-heels in love with Miss Benfold who was in charge of PE, and every time she showed herself in the yard when he was on duty, he grabbed somebody's football and started dribbling like an overweight steer to try and impress her, the big joke being he couldn't play football for monkey nuts.

Billy could hear the five past nine bus from

Crag End whining up the hill outside the school. What the heck was going on, he wondered. Why hadn't they been called in for Assembly?

Next thing he knew, the ball whizzed in at about ninety miles an hour from somewhere out in the middle of the field, whacking against the wall of Miss Benfold's classroom (missing a window by about three trillionths of an inch), and rebounded down into the yard to bounce off Little Chuff's empty bonce and frighten the life out of him – which amused Bozzy that much, he fell off his crutches.

Emma helped him up, then ran up to the corner of Miss Benfold's classroom where she could keep a watch out for Mr Fixby. After a quick shufty she nodded to Billy that the coast was clear.

Billy shouted, 'Okay, Elvis!' and a second later Elvis came over the wall and dropped down into the yard.

They were just getting into the game again when, all of a sudden, Butch barged in among them. Perhaps all his 'horses' had collapsed with splayed knees. Or maybe he'd just come through another phase in his varied and brilliant career.

At any rate he knocked Joey over and began to steer the ball towards the goal, roughly speaking: everything Butch did was roughly speaking.

He was just about to shoot when Emma nipped in and took the ball neatly off his toe. It was too late for Butch to stop his swing through:

he ended flat on his back. Meanwhile Emma had taken the ball away from the goal. She turned back in towards it, looking for her partner, Joey, when Butch – who had regained his feet – charged in from behind and deliberately tripped her up.

Emma grabbed the ball as she lay there. She scrambled to her feet and placed the football on the spot.

'Penalty!' she said.

'Who sez?'

'I do.'

'What do you know about football?' Butch wanted to know. 'You're only a girl!'

'I know a lot more than you do, Butcher,' Emma said. 'You're only an idiot!'

That was another amazing thing about Emma Ward. She wasn't afraid of Butcher. She wasn't afraid of anybody.

'That was never a penalty,' said Slattery. 'Fair charge, that.'

Slattery was the world's Number One Creep.

'I agree,' said Butch, grinning.

Emma had meanwhile run back to take her penalty. She was just waiting for Bozzy to adjust his crutches. As she began her run up, Butch, who was standing beside the ball, kicked it away and jeered at her.

'That was stupid!' said Billy.

He wished he had bitten his tongue off the minute he said it. But the words just came out. Like his dad, he did like to see fair play. His dad was always in demand down at the club as a referee in pool matches and bowls tournaments.

'What did you say?' Butch asked him.

Fortunately, Billy never got the chance to answer.

The whistle blew behind him. Turning round, he saw Mr Fixby standing at the entrance to the school. The way his eyes glowed, and the way his hands hung heavy at his sides, reminded Billy of a robot from outer space that had been sent to police the universe in a film he'd seen recently.

When everybody was dead still and quiet, Mr Fixby said:

'You will *not* go to your classroom when I blow the whistle this morning. You will go straight to the hall for Assembly instead!'

He blew a second blast on his whistle. Everyone in the yard moved towards him like obedient earthlings.

Chapter 5

You could see it wasn't an ordinary Assembly.
They had even brought the Infants over from
the other building.

'Now I've called you all together this morning
for a special Assembly because I have a rather
special message for you,' the Headmaster said,
'from the Police.'

The Headmaster was Mr Starr. He was a
small neat man, with silver hair and false teeth
that sometimes rattled. But although he was so
ancient and decrepit, he could still kick a ball
around when he wanted to.

Yonks ago, Mr Starr had played football for
the Athletic. He had been in the team when
they won the FA Cup, and there was still a
picture of him in the changing room. Steven –
who had played for the Athletic himself before
moving down to Barnsley – had told Billy all
about it.

'Now, I don't want anybody to get all silly and
excited—' said Mr Starr, and no sooner had the
words left his mouth than everybody got all silly
and excited.

All round Billy heads started swivelling back
and forth, as if they were suddenly keen on
detaching themselves from their shoulders. A
peculiar whinging sound started coming from
the front two rows where the Infants were.

When Billy glanced at Elvis, sitting next to him, he saw he had crossed his eyes and was sticking his tongue out.

Nothing unusual in that, of course.

'Now, when we're all quite certain we have recovered ourselves,' said Mr Starr, 'I shall continue.' Everybody heard his teeth rattle.

Some boys in the top class behind Billy started a coughing fit and Mr Fixby began a slow, lumbering walk up the side of the hall, eyes blazing: he looked more than ever like a robot.

But Billy knew that what Mr Starr was about to say must be really important because Mrs Drury had stopped her knitting. Billy had never seen her do that before, not in Assembly.

'That's better,' said Mr Starr, after a moment or two, 'much better,' though it wasn't, not a lot. 'Now perhaps some of you saw the local news item on the telly last night about that dog?'

A tremor of excitement passed through the rows of cross-legged children, and Elvis hissed 'Rabies!' in Billy's ear. Turning to look at him, Billy was aware that his friend's face was streaked with a vague kind of foody substance, as if he had been endeavouring to eat spaghetti in a gale-force wind.

Nothing unusual in that, either.

'Well, apparently,' said Mr Starr, after a slight rattle, 'there is just a possibility that this ... er ... dog is heading in our – rattle – direction, and the Police have phoned me to say—'

36

'AAAAAAAAAAAARRRRGGGHHHHHH!'

It was an Infant in Mrs Wendover's class who had stood up and screamed: a small insignificant-looking kid wearing a Muppet T-shirt with good old friendly Kermit pictured on the back; a kid who looked no more substantial than a reject in a cornflake factory. It was just amazing, Billy thought, what an awful lot of noise a tiny body could make when it wanted to. When the kid screamed again, all the house shields ranged along the walls seemed to tremble.

'Oh dear, oh dear, oh dear – what *have* we done now?' asked Mr Starr, rattling. 'Whatever is the matter with that child – rattle?'

'Please, sir,' said another Infant, struggling to her feet. 'Please sir, he's scared of dogs!'

'Please, sir, Mr Starr, *I* am, and all!' announced a third Infant.

By now there were half a dozen on their feet, hands waving wildly in the air like triffid stings poised to strike.

'Please, sir, me mam sez I was bit wi' a dog when I was little in me pram!' said a fourth.

'So was I, sir!' shouted a fifth.

By now Kermit the Frog had decided he had had enough and was going home to see his mammy, pronto; but halfway along the row he tripped over and fell on top of another Infant, and made her cry and all.

'Oh dear, oh dear!' shouted Mr Starr, looking a bit agitated by now. 'Mrs Wendover, could you possibly attend to that child!'

Mrs Wendover, an ample woman built like a tank and heavily armoured in tweeds and double-knit wool, moved swiftly into action in her role as Head of Infants. She soon had the wailing Kermit clamped safely and suffocatingly to her expansive chest, and had exited with him as if from a towering inferno in the direction of the First Aid cupboard.

'Now I do hope we're not going to be silly children, not in our school,' said Mr Starr after coughing thrice. Peace was more or less restored in the two rows of Infants, though one or two frightened squeaks still came from that direction. He waited until a second onslaught of coughing ceased from the top class at the back. Elvis was nipping the bottom of the kid in front of him, but he didn't dare move in case Mr Fixby saw him. 'I'm sure we can leave silly behaviour to other schools,' said Mr Starr. '*We* know better.' The kid Elvis was nipping suddenly jumped and Mr Fixby saw him at once. He didn't say anything. He just nodded twice and smiled at the poor mutt. Everybody knew what that meant. 'Now,' said Mr Starr, 'I'm sure you've all heard the expression "Better safe than sorry" – haven't you?'

'I have, sir,' said Pat Shufflebotham, shoving her hand up. She was Little Chuff's big sister. She was always answering questions when she wasn't supposed to. The pair of them hadn't a brain between them; they hadn't half a brain.

'Well,' said Mr Starr, ignoring Pat Shufflebotham's fluttering hand as far as was humanly possible, 'I want you all to remember that little saying during the next few days, and if you happen to see this . . . er . . . big grey dog they were on about in the news, I want you to go straight home and tell your mums and dads about it – all right? Do I make myself perfectly – rattle – clear?'

'YES-MISTER-STARR,' answered the children in solid unison, all except for Pat Shufflebotham who was still fluttering her hand about.

'It isn't that the Police know for certain that this dog is dangerous, you know,' said Mr Starr. 'I don't want you to run away with that silly idea. Not at all. We don't want any panic. This big grey dog may be perfectly harmless for all we know. But we can't be absolutely certain about that just yet. Not one hundred per cent certain. So, until we are, the Police are advising you to keep well away from the animal. Don't attempt to pat it or anything of that kind. Don't offer it any food. Do I make myself clear?'

'YES-MISTER-STARR.'

'Good. Just remember that expression: Better safe than sorry. I want you to make your way to your classrooms quickly and quietly when Mr Fixby dismisses your class. That will be all.'

He leapt athletically down from the dais and vanished into the short tunnel that led to his office.

Mrs Drury, who amazingly enough had still not resumed her knitting, noticed that Pat Shufflebotham's hand was still flying at full-mast.

'What is it you want to ask, dear?' she asked.

Pat Shufflebotham looked dazed. She looked up and realized her hand was up in the air. She hauled it down.

'Forgotten, miss,' she said.

Chapter 6

As soon as Elvis entered their classroom he shouted, 'RABIES!': then he started foaming at the mouth, leaping about all over the shop, and trying to sink his gnashers into people's legs. Most of the girls started screaming and acting daft, and one or two even climbed on their desk tops. Emma Ward just laughed at him and went to the back of the classroom with Billy to watch him feed the fish. It was his turn this week.

Samantha Soskiss was the only one who ignored Elvis altogether. As he lolloped towards her down the aisle, head rolling, drooling gallons of spit, she carried on opening her pencil case and setting out all the paraphernalia from it, as if nothing whatever was the matter. Even when Elvis bit her, just above her white ankle socks, she carried on sharpening her pencil.

That was just like Samantha Soskiss. She was what Elvis's dad called a 'workaholic', a person who wasn't happy unless they were working. Mr Potter felt sorry for such people. He said they were to be pitied more than anything else.

Last year, when they were in Miss Benfold's class, Samantha Soskiss had actually asked to go to the library and work on her project on Florence Nightingale on the last day of term – when all the rest of them were playing games and having quizzes.

'He's a right nutcase!' Emma said to Billy.

'I know.'

Billy watched the fish rising from the depths of their tank, mouths gaping to take the food. It was amazing how little you had to give them. Give them too much and they could easily die.

Mrs Drury hadn't wanted him to have his turn. She reckoned he and Elvis had put the superglue on the seats in the boys' bogs last week. It hadn't been them, not this time. But she always accused Elvis of everything, and Billy had happened to be with him at the time. He wouldn't have got his turn if Emma hadn't suggested they should put it to the vote. Mrs Drury was always telling them how she believed in democracy because the Ancient Greeks invented it — Elvis was always saying she *was* one of the Ancient Greeks — so she had no option: twenty-nine had voted for Billy and only three against.

Billy handed the fish food to Emma to let her finish off the job, and just as he did so there was a loud *thwack* behind them.

Samantha Soskiss had brought the edge of her solid wood pencilcase down on the mad dog's napper. It yelped, rolled over on its back, and stuck its paws up in the air.

Everybody laughed and crowded round to have a good look. So only Billy and Emma noticed when Mrs Drury appeared in the doorway.

'WHAT ON EARTH IS GOING ON HERE?'

Everybody scattered back to their places, all

except Elvis. He remained with his paws stuck
up in the air.

'What on earth are you doing, you stupid
child?'

'Me, miss? Lyin' on me back, miss. Why,
miss?'

'Get up, you ridiculous idiot! Get up!' Then
she glared at Emma and Billy. 'And what are
you doing, Emma Ward?

'Helping Billy feed the fish, miss.'

'I thought *you* were the one that was so keen
for him to have his turn? Sit down at once. And
you as well, Billy Robinson, we don't want the
fish over-feeding.'

She glared at them until they were all back

in their places. A pause. Then she marched over to her desk and cast her knitting on to it – as if the half-finished cardigan for her grandson that she'd spent the last three years on was absolutely of no importance whatsoever.

Mrs Drury was not Billy's favourite teacher. He often wished he was back in Miss Benfold's. But when it came to acting he had to admit that Mrs Drury was in the Oscar category.

'All I can say, 3D, is that I am very disappointed in you. *Terribly* disappointed.'

And she looked it as well. She could look anything she wanted.

It was no wonder she was the leading light in the St Luke's Church Amateur Theatrical Society – which Elvis called the St Crook's Hammerchewers. Billy's grandma, who was a keen church-goer, had taken her to see three of their plays.

In the first play Mrs Drury had been a bossy headmistress. In the second she was a bossy vicar's wife. And in the third she played an ordinary bossy lady who had murdered her husband with weedkiller and then hid him in the grandfather clock. She'd been good in all three parts.

It wasn't her fault that the third play had gone wrong at the end. What happened was, they couldn't get a proper grandfather clock so they made one out of cardboard, and halfway through Act Three the clock fell over and everybody saw that the dead husband had gone. Billy's grandma told him afterwards that the fellar playing the part had got bored with being dead and had nipped off for a fag instead.

'*Terribly, terribly* disappointed,' she said. That was one of her few weaknesses as an actress, Billy had noticed. Whenever she hit on a good line she was bound to repeat it. '*Most* disappointed,' she said, then paused.

'Please, miss?'

She glared at Cloughy: she hated it when people interrupted one of her pauses.

'What is it, Clough?'

'Please, miss, 'as it really got rabies?'

'I *beg* your pardon, Clough?'

'That dog, miss. Has it really got rabies?'

'Whoever suggested such a thing, Clough? Did anyone in this room hear Mr Starr even suggest such a thing? *I* didn't. And I certainly washed *my* ears out this morning.'

As she spoke she glanced towards Elvis, as if insinuating that *he* hadn't. Which was probably quite true. The only time Elvis washed his ears out nowadays was when they went to the baths for swimming. It wasn't altogether his fault. They were going through a bathroom crisis at the Potters' house. A few months back Mr Potter had won a load of money on a greyhound called The Palooka and had their old bath ripped out. They ordered a posh new one, a suite called Plaza de Roma, but before it was installed Mr Potter lost all his winnings on a racehorse called Sulky Sam.

'So we don't want to hear any more of that ridiculous idea,' said Mrs Drury.

Actually, the rabies idea wasn't really that ridiculous. The same black thought had leapt straight to the back of Billy's mind while Mr Starr had been speaking.

The week before there'd been a film on telly about a woman who had smuggled her chihuahua back from France in her handbag and, in less than a fortnight, there was rabies all over England because, unbeknown to the woman, her dog had already been infected by a French fox.

In one scene all these mad dogs were trying to get at a woman in a car. Billy had been so scared that the following morning he thought twice about stroking next-door's cat when it came along the backyard wall for its usual bit of attention.

'As far as we know, the facts are these,' said Mrs Drury, sitting down at her desk and opening her register. 'The dog may or may not be dangerous. All we know for certain is that it is very large and probably grey.'

'Sounds like *The Hound of the Baskervilles*, miss,' said Butch.

'I beg your pardon, Butcher? I'm surprised you've even heard of *The Hound of the Baskervilles*. As far as I'm concerned *The Hound of the Baskervilles* is a work of literature.'

'I know, miss. It was on telly last Christmas.'

'Aaaahh!' said Mrs Drury, stretching the word out till it was ten miles long. 'That explains it, Butcher. For one awful moment I thought you'd actually read a book!'

47

All of her cronies laughed. None of the boys did. If they had, Butch would have beaten them down to pulp in the bogs at morning break, then flushed them down the lav.

'I don't suppose you know who wrote it, Butcher?'

And all the members of the Drury Swots Club started waving their flippers in the air.

Billy knew who had written it, of course. But he wasn't going to put his hand up. That was the trouble with being in Mrs Drury's. You always felt rotten when you put your hand up. It hadn't been like that in Miss Benfold's.

Instead, he glanced down at what Elvis was drawing on a sheet of paper he ought to have used for his graph work yesterday: a ginormous hairy dog with spiky teeth, and round its feet millions of pin men shooting arrows at it and flinging their useless spears.

'Miss, was it Enid Blyton?'

A few snortles and guffaws round him made Butch go redder than he was already.

'Miss!'

'Miss!'

'Miss!'

The noise reminded Billy of a film he'd seen at Elvis's. All these arrows were flying through the air, shoals and shoals of them like thin black killer-fish, and all these knights were clonking to the ground. All the knights had horses and they were clad in cast iron, but they still couldn't beat the bowmen, because the bowmen were British.

'Alison?'

'Miss, was it Doyle Carte, miss?'

'Unfortunately not, but a good try. Take half a house point.'

'Miss, we're doing a nopra by Doyle Carte next summer, miss.'

'I'm afraid that's not quite right either, dear,' said Mrs Drury.

'It is, miss, honest, miss, 'cos I've gorra non-speaking part, miss, because of me tap dancing, as a Japanese maiden.'

Alison Fretwell was always going on about her tap dancing. Elvis used to say she was tapped.

'Fu-man-poo, the silent menace,' Elvis said now, under his breath.

'How very interesting, Alison dear,' Mrs Drury said as she turned her attention elsewhere. 'Samantha?'

'Conan Doyle, miss.'

'Soskiss strikes again!' muttered Elvis under his breath.

'Quite right! Conan Doyle. *Not* Doyle Carte. One house point. And does anyone happen to know the name of the famous detective—'

'Miss!'

'Miss!'

'Miss!'

Once more arrows flew through the air and knights clonked to the ground.

'You again, Samantha dear.'

'Sherlock Holmes, miss.'

'*Two* house points!' said Mrs Drury, beaming

49

at her star pupil.

'Rather 'ave house *pints*, miss,' muttered Elvis, rather too loudly.

'Pardon me, Potter? Did I understand you to speak?'

'Me, miss? When, miss? No, miss. Honest, miss.'

The Great Detective was just about to start her investigation into the Case of the Lying Nutter, when there was a tap at the door and a boy from Miss Benfold's, Adrian Belcher, came in.

'Please, Mrs Drury, Miss Benfold wants to know, miss, if Patricia Shufflebotham's in school today, miss?'

Mrs Drury – and nearly all the other thirty-two of them – swivelled round in their seats to make absolutely certain that Pat Shufflebotham was still with them.

Pat Shufflebotham went a pale shade of white and giggled. She always did when too many people looked at her. She stuck her thumb in her mouth and a smile of worry flitted over her face.

'Well, what if she is?' Mrs Drury asked the boy.

'Please, miss, what it is is, Miss Benfold wants to know if she brought her little brother to school or not this morning, miss.'

Mrs Drury looked inquiringly at Pat Shufflebotham.

There was a look of blank bewilderment on the girl's face.

50

'Well, Patricia?' asked Mrs Drury. 'Can you remember if you brought Ernest to school this morning?' She went down the aisle and knelt down beside her. She took one of her hands. 'Patricia? Did you bring him, or not?'

Everybody in the class knew what was happening. Patricia Shufflebotham was always going like this. She sort of locked herself up in silence. She wouldn't speak for ages. Or perhaps she *couldn't* speak.

'Patricia, darling?'

Even before she came to school she used to do it. She used to stand at the bottom of Bertha, or by the swings in the rec in front of Chapel Row, and wouldn't speak to anybody.

'Are you trying to remember?'

Some of the teachers didn't know about her and they could get snappy. But Mrs Drury had never got nasty with her, not up to just.

Emma Ward put up her hand but Mrs Drury just ignored her.

'Why don't you tell me?'

'Miss?' said Billy. 'Please, miss, she *did* bring him to school, because he was watching us have a kickabout in the yard.'

Mrs Drury looked at him as if he'd just broken the Ten Commandments. 'I thought we didn't call out in this classroom, Billy Robinson. Thank you for the information, but we can wait for Patricia to reply. We are in no hurry, thank you.'

She turned back to Patricia Shufflebotham. 'Well, Patricia? Try to remember, dear. Did you

51

Chapter 7

They found Little Chuff at dinnertime. He'd hid himself in the caretaker's coalshed, but a bit of the strap from his Amazing Spiderman bag was left hanging outside the door, so somebody noticed it.

He'd got scared in Assembly after what Mr Starr said about the dog, and he didn't want to go home because his dad was at work and his mam always went to the Bingo Club on Wednesdays because the cards were half-price.

He had to go to see Mr Starr after his dinner, but he didn't get punished or anything like that. Mr Starr never punished the Chuffs for anything: he'd taught their mam and dad.

The mist had thickened up all day, seeming to pile up against the classroom windows by late morning, as if trying to shut them in forever, and by dinnertime making it impossible to see halfway across the yard. As Billy walked home along Station Road all the buses and cars had full headlights on, even though it was only four o'clock.

He went to feed the hens and pigeons as soon as he got home, not bothering to eat his jam sandwich and have his drink of pop. He wanted to get the job over and done with before darkness really set in.

Not that he was really scared. He had Dot

with him, and if anything was wrong she would at least give him fair warning. She'd probably throw her life away to save him, Billy thought, if the worst came to the worst. She was that kind of dog. She hadn't a lot of sense. In fact, none at all. But she *was* faithful, true and loving.

The thought reassured him as he climbed up the back street and then went through the rickety old gate that led to the allotments.

There were forty or fifty allotments covering the slope above the colliery terraces, and a maze of winding paths jiggling their way between ramshackle fences that leaned this way and that.

Dot was out of sight in the mists ahead of him, her clumsy feet scattering stones from the path as they climbed. Billy knew she would soon let him know if there was anything up there – anything wrong.

Trouble was, his dad's allotment was situated right at the very top. You could scream your head off up there, you could scream blue murder, and nobody would hear a dicky-bird. Especially with this cotton wool mist all round you.

But there seemed to be nothing wrong when they reached the allotment. Billy let Dot in first and stood by the gate watching her. He wondered if he would throw away *his* life to save hers, if the huge grey dog suddenly appeared out of the dense hawthorn hedge that formed the top edge of the allotments.

He had a bucket with him, to carry up the food and water and to take back the eggs: he might be able to use that as a weapon. It might help. He doubted it, though.

In any case, as a human being perhaps he ought to take it for granted that an animal's life should be sacrificed to preserve his own, like the animals Mrs Drury was always telling them about that were forced to smoke cigarettes all day. Billy wasn't sure about that.

But in any case, Dot's curiosity, as she sniffed among the plant pots and along the hedge, seemed nothing out of the ordinary. Eventually, when she slipped through a gap in the hawthorns to investigate the gorse-covered slope beyond as she normally did, he let the gate swing to behind him and went to see to the hens.

After gathering the eggs he shut the pop-hole, and leaned a heavy stone against it, just to make sure. Then he saw to the pigeons. He was glad their hut was padlocked nowadays, at least tonight. His dad had put a padlock on only a few months ago, for the first time in his life. Some vandals had broken into another fellar's hut and done some damage. Normally it was a nuisance fiddling with a lock, but at least the Ghost Dog wouldn't be able to pick a lock.

Or would it?

Apparently it couldn't. The only occupants of the pigeon hut were the pigeons themselves. And they seemed all right.

When he came outside again he checked the lock, then double-checked it. He must be getting

nervous! Elvis would have laughed at him if he had known.

He stood for a moment in the strange half-darkness. From where he was, standing by the cold frame, he could just make out his dad's Brussels sprouts: in the mist they could easily have been mistaken for weird aliens advancing through a poisonous smokescreen.

Then he noticed a strange thing. Apart from the drip, drip of moisture in the hedge, there was no sound at all.

No sound from the railway yards down in the valley, yet it wasn't yet five o'clock. Shunting engines would still be hard at work. Trucks would be juddering back and forth.

No sound from the cars and lorries, either, as they nosed their way along Station Road, though Billy knew that soon folks would be parping on their horns because they wanted to get home for their teas.

He couldn't even hear Dot, and that was saying something. Although she was a menace, she wasn't – like Elvis's Fu-Man-Poo – a silent one. You could normally hear her coming a mile off, she was that clumsy.

'Dot!'

Drip, drip: that was all.

'Dotty! Come here!'

It occurred to him that she might have done something stupid. Beyond the hawthorns, the ground sloped gently until it came to a sheer limestone drop of about thirty feet called the Edge which ran for about half a mile alongside the Old Line, gradually losing height until it petered out altogether just about opposite Fox-cover Wood.

Billy went towards the hedge. He called her again. He squeezed his way through the thorny gap.

'Dot, you stupid thing! Where are you?'

His voice seemed hardly to penetrate the mists. 'DOT!' He'd often seen her chasing rabbits in and out of the gorse bushes. It would be just like her to—

And then in the silence he heard her.

She was just a few yards off to his right somewhere, making her excited squeaking noises.

He felt his way towards her over the tussocky grass, manoeuvring round gorse bushes, calling her all the time.

And then at last he saw her.

She was standing practically still, ears pricked forward, nose sniffing the air, one silly paw held just above the grass and trembling.

He grabbed her collar.

At that moment the mist in front of them cleared for a moment in a breath of wind and Billy saw – nothing. The stupid animal seemed to be sniffing at nothing at all.

Chapter 8

The Ghost Dog didn't have rabies. They told you
that on the *Looking Out* programme that night.

Lord La-de-dah was interviewing what he
called 'a police spokesman', a solid grey-looking
man who looked as if he lived entirely on thick
porridge and tatie-water. He reminded Billy of
the school computer because after every question he waited six months before he started his
reply.

'Is a police spokesman a fellar that meks
spokes for the wheels on police cars, Dad?' Billy
asked.

His dad ignored him.

'Shut your mouth, Our Billy,' said his mam,
'and do speak properly.'

Billy knew what was up with her. She was on
tenterhooks waiting to go down to the phone
again. They *had* been down the night before,
Mrs Potter had been right about that: and she'd
been right about them phoning Sandra.

Which had puzzled Billy at first, because
Steven and Sandra didn't have a phone. But his
mam told him Sandra had sent the number of
the Workmen's Club in Barnsley and what time
to ring through to her. Pretty brainy, that, Billy
had thought. He hadn't realized his sister had
any brains before.

'So we can assure our good local folk on that

point, actually, can we?' asked Lord La-de-dah.

'Substantively, yes,' said the Police Computer. 'On the basis of saliva tests taken so far, together with relevant information already available and appertaining to this juncture in time, it is reasonable to assume so.'

'What's that supposed to mean when it's all there?' asked Billy's dad.

'It means the dog hasn't got it, Dad,' Billy explained to him.

'Don't be cheeky to your dad,' his mother said sharply. 'Do you think he's ignorant or something?'

Billy didn't answer that one.

'But there is still some danger, is there, I suppose?'

'Considering circumstantial evidence and experience gained from past similar experience, it is hard to reply in the negative,' said the Computer.

'What's he want to talk like that for, Dad?' Billy asked.

'He talks like that, Billy, because he's properly educated,' said his mother.

'In my opinion, he's after promotion, son,' said his dad. 'Likely as not he's out to impress the high-ups. It's no good talking like me and your mother, you know, if you want to get on in life. If you want to get on, you have to learn to mek your mouth go a bit.'

'And are we to understand that this Ghost Dog is now travelling in a south-westerly direction?'

'That's towards us,' said Billy's dad. He reached for his pipe and baccy.

'That is correct.' The Police Computer happened to nod his head at precisely the moment Billy's dad spoke, as if in agreement with him. 'According to information received in the last hour, the animal – or perhaps I should say *some* animal – has been observed by a variety of sources travelling, approximately speaking, in the direction of Belton Buildings.'

'What did I tell yer!' asked Billy's dad looking round at them as if he'd just won the jackpot on

a TV game show. A second later his match burnt his finger, and he dropped it on the mat and had to stamp it out with his foot. 'Hell and damnation!' he said.

'What time are we going for that phone, Dick? It's nearly time now,' asked Billy's mam. She got up and went out into the kitchen to fetch the floorcloth.

'And are we given to understand that the animal was seen by an engine driver, actually?'

'Correct.'

'And that was on the main line from Durham to Darlington, was it?'

'Correct.'

'Heading south, I believe?'

'Correct.'

'Know who he sounds like, Dad?'

'That fellar on *Masterbrain*?'

'Correct!' said Billy.

'Shut up!' said his mother, coming back in with the floorcloth.

'Correct,' said the Police Computer in answer to another question.

'I wonder if you could possibly elaborate on that?'

'Certainly. According to information at our disposal at this present juncture in time, the train was proceeding south from Durham City at an approximate speed of fifty-three miles an hour when the driver – of the engine, that is – leaned out of his cab and perceived – or *said* he perceived, according to *my* information – a large dog – or it could have been a creature – staring at him from the embankment on the up-line side.'

'And I believe that, in actual fact, he was able to supply some details?'

'Correct.'

'Here we go again!' said Billy's dad.

'Correct!' said Billy.

'I'll give you a fourpenny one in a minute, young man!' said his mam.

'Making allowances for the heavy mist at the time,' said the Police Computer, 'which we must do, together with the relative speed of the train, which we must also do, and remembering that the accompanying guard at the time was unable to state that he saw anything untoward at all, the driver described the animal – or whatever – as being between three to four feet at the shoulder, grey, with a shaggy coat, and staring eyes.'

'Sounds like me grandma!' said Billy.

'Sounds more like a donkey to me, actually!' giggled Lord La-de-dah.

'Don't you dare talk about your grandma like that!' said Billy's mam.

'If you ask me,' said Billy's dad, addressing the telly, 'the whole lot of you's donkeys on that programme!'

'Are we going for that phone, or not, Dick? She did say twenty to.'

The Police Computer had paused again. Billy wondered if he was reversing his tapes. Or perhaps he was doing a data search?

His dad squirmed round in his chair by the

fireplace.

'I've told you lass, there's no need to get aeriated over this matter. It's not a bit of good mekkin' a mountain out of a molehill, you know.'

'I don't think you appreciate the gravity of the situation, Dick,' said Billy's mam.

'What situation, Mam?' asked Billy.

Worry was written plainly all over her face.

'Never you mind, Billy!' she snapped at him. Then she suddenly stood up and charged across to the telly and switched it off. 'I can't stand that racket any more!' she said.

'I'd best get me coat,' said Billy's dad, standing up. He went into the kitchen. Billy heard him getting some coins from the small change tin they kept on the mantelpiece. He came back into the room with his coat and hat on. 'Ready, lass?'

'Can I come with you this time, Mam?' Billy asked.

'No, Billy.'

'What for?'

She didn't reply.

'You stop in and keep the fire on, lad,' his dad said. 'We'll not be a minute.'

'That comedy show'll be on after the news,' his mam said, 'the one you always enjoy.'

'Don't fancy it tonight.'

'Don't be soft, Our Billy, you know it's your favourite programme.'

'I fancy going round to Elvis's instead.'

His mother gave him one of her *by-gum-*

young-man-I've-just-about-had-a-bellyful-of-you! looks. She sniffed, but didn't say anything. It was quite clear that she thought Billy was just being awkward on purpose: and she was right.

'Just mek sure you're sharp back then,' his dad said. 'We don't want you round the Potters' till all hours of the night.' He took Dot's lead out of his pocket. 'We might as well tek the dog with us, shall we, lass? Give her a bit of a run.'

Dot jumped up in excitement and made Billy's dad stagger back, nearly knocking the potted plant over.

'She is a clumsy animal, that dog!' said Billy's mam. 'I sometimes wish we'd never got her. What'll we do with her while we're phoning?'

'I'll take her round to Elvis's with me, if you like,' Billy said.

'What for?' his mother asked. 'So you can give her fleas? I don't want no dog coming back in this house with fleas – no thank you!'

Billy's mam was always going on about the Potters having fleas and being mucky. Just because they kept their hens under the kitchen table and didn't have a vacuum cleaner. In actual fact, they *did* have a vacuum cleaner, only it hadn't worked for a year or two. Mr Potter never had time to mend it.

And in Billy's opinion it would have been better if his mother – who was supposed to be keen on education and that sort of thing – sat down and read a book now and then, for a change, instead of flying round with a duster in

66

her hand and getting people to clean their shoes and polish their teeth every five minutes of the day.

Mrs Potter was always with her head in a book. She was particularly fond of what Billy's grandma called 'hysterical romances'. Mrs Potter once said to Billy, 'I'm not going to be a slave to my house, Billy, not like some folks I could mention!' And she wasn't. As soon as the sun shone, she was outside their fronts sitting on a buffet getting her knees brown, and showing all her legs. That was the reason why a lot of people said the Potters' house was the sort of place where you wiped your feet when you came out, instead of going in.

He waited until his mam and dad were well out of the way before he switched on the telly.

His favourite comedian was dressed in short trousers and kept falling off the stage. He was supposed to be Adolf Hitler, who started the War. He had a stuffed dog under his arm and his trousers kept falling down. A woman with hardly any clothes on came in and handed him a letter – and that reminded Billy of the letter from his sister.

He went in the kitchen and had a good look for it on the mantelpiece. He even stood on a chair. But he couldn't find it. It was rotten not being told what was going on. It wasn't right.

When he went back into the other room, the comedian was chasing the woman with hardly any clothes on. His trousers fell down and tripped him up. He wore silk underpants, with a Union Jack across his bottom.

Billy was tempted to stay.

But he didn't want his mam to catch him enjoying the telly. And he was sick of being treated like a kid.

So he switched off the telly and went round to Elvis's.

It was dark as he went up the backs and he wished they'd left Dot with him for company. But, in actual fact – as La-de-dah would have said – there was no sign of the Ghost Dog, not that night.

Chapter 9

The Ghost Dog appeared the following night, when they were all playing Tally-ho.

Up in the allotments was a good place to hide. It was pitch dark up there, out of reach of the street lamps. In somebody's garden was out of bounds, but there were still masses of places to hide in the pathways that zig-zagged and crossed like the twisting of a maze.

But Billy didn't hide up in the allotments that night. Nobody did. Not even Elvis was daft enough.

Butch's team were on-block at the top of Victoria. That meant they were supposed to have their heads down and their eyes shut as they counted to a hundred while Elvis's team ran away and hid – *supposed*!

Billy went belting down Wolsley backs, Joey White and Cloughy running just ahead of him. Joey split off from them, and climbed down into a dustbin and then lowered the lid down over his head.

'Nighty-nighty!' they heard him say.

A few yards further, when they weren't even halfway down the backs, they heard Butch yell: 'FIFTY!'

Butch had a unique way of counting when he was on-block. It went more or less like this: one, two, twenty, thirty-eight, forty-nine, FIFTY!

And he was the best runner. *And* a lot of kids gave themselves up, *and* told him where their mates were hid – just to get in his good books.

'ONE HUNDRED!'

'—and eighty!' shouted Cloughy, clattering on down the backs.

Billy had screeched to a halt by somebody's backyard gate. He clambered up it, using the sneck for a toe-hold, then flattened himself out like a thin squirt of toothpaste on the wall above it.

'COMING! READY OR NOT!'

Howls and shouts started flowing down the backs as three or four hunters came after them. Almost straight away they started kicking the dustbins and lifting lids, so Billy knew they must have been cheating, must have had their big lugholes poked round the corner of Wolsley backs, it was too misty for them to have seen anything.

'Out!' Butch shouted. 'Out of that trash-can, Joey!'

'You must've been lookin', man!'

'Could smell you a mile off!' said Butch. 'Where's Robbo?'

'Search me, man.'

'Howay, lads!'

Billy pressed himself down into the bricks as the hunters ran past making their daft WHUP-WHUP sounds. He thought about dropping down into the yard. But that would have been cheating. It was just lucky the kitchen behind him didn't have its lights on.

Joey

The shouts grew fainter, and almost died away. They must be searching the rec by now. He heard Daz helping Joey out of the bin. They both got the giggling fits when it fell over with a clatter. They were giggling all the way up the backs as Daz escorted him back to the prisoners' base.

Two minutes passed. Billy was beginning to think they'd never find him there. The light went on in the kitchen behind him. A chap came out to fill the coal. He was whistling the theme tune from a cops-and-robbers show on the telly. He shut the coalhouse door and went back in again.

Terry in the show on the telly always reminded Billy of Steven. They were both pretty tough. They were both pretty soft in the head as well.

He wondered what was going on with their Sandra and Steven. The night before, Mrs Potter had seemed to think it was Steven's fault.

'So there's nothing wrong down in Barnsley, is there?' she had said.

'Not that I know of, Mrs Potter.'

He knew she was trying to pump him for information. But Billy had seen too many crime films to be fooled like that.

'Want another chocolate?' she asked, offering him the box.

'Only, Steven was a funny 'un before he was married,' she said.

'He was that,' said Mr Potter. 'And marrying's not going to change a fellar like that!'

Billy had wondered what they meant, and that had made him pause just a little before he took the chocolate; and it was possible that Mr and Mrs Potter had both noticed that tiny pause: they certainly seemed to.

Now he wondered why.

And it was while he was wondering that he heard the howl.

It could have been a dog. Just an ordinary dog. It was probably in somebody's backyard, wanting to be let in the house to watch the telly. But he couldn't see the sense in taking too many chances.

He scrambled down, his foot feeling for the sneck, then ran towards the lights at the bottom of Wolsley, his feet clattering noisily on the cobbles.

He turned the corner at ninety miles an hour and ran slap bang into Butch's chest. It was like hitting the Great Wall of China.

Cloughy was already caught.

'Where's Elvis?' said Butch.

'Haven't a clue,' said Billy.

Which was true at the time.

But ten minutes later, when Billy and the rest of Elvis's team were in the prisoners' base at the top of Victoria, it was much clearer to Billy where Elvis was. It was much clearer to all of them. He was either up in the allotments or down the path that led to the Old Line.

'He can't be up there!' said Butch, looking towards the allotment gate.

'I'll go up if you like, Butch,' said Emma Ward.

'I've told you, Wardy! You're not playing and that's final!'

'Let her join in, man, Butch,' said Joey.

'What's up with her, anyroad?' asked Billy.

'What's up with her is she's a girl – that's what's up wi' her!' Butch whacked his stick against the rails of the allotments fence and then walked towards the path that led down to the Old Line. 'Two of you come wi' me, the rest stand guard.'

But Butch never even started down the path because they heard the sound of something coming up from the darkness towards him. The sound of something heavy, scattering stones as it ran, something breathing heavily as it climbed.

Butch was frozen into stillness. They all were.

Then Elvis shot into view.

'It's back down there!' he shouted. 'That Ghost Dog! It's real big!' At first they didn't believe him. Butch even took a step forward to capture him, but then they all saw something large and grey coming out of the mist towards them, and they all heard a low, long growl.

And they all ran then.

Chapter 10

There was nobody in the house when Billy got back. He hammered and hammered on the front door, but nobody answered, and neither did Dot bark. They must have gone down to the blinking telephone again!

He had to go all the way down the fronts and then up the backs. On the way he looked in at the telephone kiosk, but it was empty, so he thought they must have finished and gone home themselves.

He shouted for his mam and dad as he started up the backs, in case they were just ahead of him. But the fog refused his words and pushed them back into his mouth again.

He took a deep breath. Up to now he'd heard doors slamming shut behind people as they dived indoors to safety, but that had stopped now. He must be the only one left out. His heart jumped when something large and white loomed up ahead of him, but it was only somebody's sheet left out on a line. He was too scared to laugh at himself. He took a deep breath instead.

When he pushed open the backyard gate, he saw that they had left the kitchen light on and he was pleased about that, though it did surprise him. It wasn't like his mam to leave lights blazing on in the house. She was always going on about saving money.

It surprised him and all to find the back door locked. If they were just popping out for five minutes, they usually left it open.

He opened the coalhouse door wide before he put his hand in to get the key off the hook but, even with the light from the kitchen window, he couldn't see an inch into the blackness. He slammed the door shut fast as soon as he had the key, then dropped the bent nail over the hasp to fasten it shut.

As soon as he pushed open the back door he heard a *bump* noise from the other room.

'Dot? It's only me.' He stood there, listening. Nothing. He called her again. She didn't come. His heart was racing like anything. This is just daft, he thought to himself. He closed the back door behind him.

And the *bump* noise came again.

He opened the back door again, quietly, carefully. He was glad he hadn't closed the backyard gate behind him.

'Anybody there?'

'It was no good being scared, he told himself. If his dad came in, he'd be ashamed of him.

Without causing a sound, he went to the kitchen table and slid open the drawer. He took the gulley knife out. That made him feel better.

He went towards the door to the other room which was a few inches open. The switch was just round the door jamb, to his left. He swapped the gulley knife into his left hand. If there *was* a burglar there – he'd better watch out. Not that it was a burglar he was really worried about. In fact, he rather hoped it *was* a burglar.

He could hear the fire making small licky-noises in the other room. Nothing else. He took a breath, then reached round the jamb with his right hand and groped for the switch, which didn't seem to be where it usually was, found it and flicked it down.

The neon light took a second before it came on with a *ping*!

There didn't seem to be anybody there. Or anything. He pushed the door wide open. There wasn't.

But everything – the sofa, the curtains, the display cabinet, telly – they all looked somehow funny under the light. Except for the small sound from the fire, everything was dead quiet in the house. He could hear that the Murrays next door were watching their telly. He also noticed that the door to the front passage was slightly open.

It was probably that which made the *bump* noise. It sometimes did that when somebody came in and shut the back door.

He felt better now. All the same, he kept the sofa between him and the passage door as he moved across the room. He picked up the poker from the fireplace as he went. He almost smiled. He realized for the first time that his legs were trembling.

'Anybody there?' he asked, looking at the passage door.

He waited for a moment, took another deep

breath. Now or never, he thought. If anybody came in now and saw him standing there, talking to the passage door with the gulley knife in one hand and the poker in the other, they'd think he was barmy.

He went to the passage door and opened it.

There was nobody there.

He switched on the stair light.

There was a picture at the top of the stairs. It was called *Between Two Fires*. It was a bit like one of Mrs Potter's hysterical romances. Two gentlemen in olden-day costumes were about to have a duel over a lady in a crinoline, who was standing behind a table looking sorry for all the trouble she was causing.

Grandma had given them that picture. Grandad had collected cigarette cards for ages, sent them off to the tobacco firm and they'd sent the picture back.

'Anybody up there?' he called, almost as a joke, though.

He could hear a faint rustling noise, probably from his bedroom. He decided to ignore it.

He left all the lights on and went and shut the back door. He locked it. He put the gulley knife back in its drawer, went back into the other room and stirred up the fire until real flames came. Then he put the poker back in its proper place.

If they didn't come back in ten minutes, he would go round to the Murray's and see if they knew what was going on.

He switched on the telly low.

Just before the adverts came on his mam and dad came back.

He had to unlock the back door to let them in.

'Where've you been, Mam?'

'The phone was vandalized, pet. We had to go right along—'

'Never mind that now,' said his dad. 'What the devil's all these lights ablaze for, Billy? And what for's the door locked?'

'Elvis Potter's seen that dog, Dad.'

'What dog?'

'That Ghost Dog.'

'Don't be soft, Our Billy. It'll be that lurcher of Tommy Harle's. It's just passed your mother and me coming down the backs.' He went into the other room and came back with the keys to the factory van. 'You ready for off now, lass? Or do you want a cup of tea?'

'I'd rather go straight away, Dick.'

'Where you going, Mam?'

'Down to Barnsley.' It was his dad that answered. 'You go and get your pyjamas and that – you'll be stopping the night with your grandma. We'll run you up there before we set off.'

'When you coming back?'

'We have no idea, son. You'll have to see to the hens in the morning – all right?'

Billy hesitated.

'Can Dot stop with me, Dad?'

His dad didn't seem to twig on at first. And then he said, 'For heaven's sake, Billy – you're surely to goodness not frightened of that dog they've been talking about? You *can't* be frightened of a dog. Not you Billy!'

Chapter 11

If Billy's grandma knew what was going on down in Barnsley, she wasn't telling Billy.

'Never trouble trouble till trouble troubles you, Billy,' she said to him. She was full of these daft sayings.

Nor was she frightened of the Ghost Dog. She didn't even bother to lock her back door after his mam and dad had gone off. That was just after the church clock struck ten.

'It can come in here this minute, pet, if it wants to,' she said, nodding at the back door. Very sensible, thought Billy. 'Just as long as its paws aren't mucky!'

She laughed into her cocoa.

Dot was curled up asleep on the clippy-mat in front of the fire, her big paws resting lightly on the legless golliwog that she liked to cuddle. Billy had remembered to bring it up for her; he'd stuffed it in his pocket at the last minute.

'Elvis Potter said it was real big, Grandma.'

'Elvis Potter's a real big liar, pet. All the Potters are real big liars. I've told you that till I'm blue in the face.'

'Are you not scared of it, though?'

'If it should walk in here this minute' (Billy wished she wouldn't keep saying that, not with the door unlocked) 'I'd give it the scraps off the

82

side in the kitchen I've been saving for their cat next door. I couldn't stand by and see an animal starve, Billy, not even if it is only a ghost.'

'Ghosts don't eat anything, Grandma.'

'Don't they, pet? I couldn't say. I never went to school as long as you.' She lit up her pipe – which had been Grandad's before he died – and threw the match on the fire. 'From what I've read in the Bible, there's no such thing as ghosts. Only Holy Ghosts. And they're not going to frighten the life out of anybody, are they?'

'I don't know, Grandma.'

'They won't.' She seemed to know all about it. She puffed smoke. 'As I say, there's no such thing as ghosts, and if one was to walk through that door this minute' (There she goes again! thought Billy) 'I'd offer a cup of cocoa and a bite to eat, same as we're having. Have you finished yours up?'

Billy looked in his mug. 'Yes.'

'Put it somewhere where you won't knock it over, pet.' She puffed blue smoke again. She was quite an expert pipe smoker, even though she hadn't taken it up as a hobby until after Grandad had died. It was quite a good pipe, practically new at the time, and she hadn't wanted to see it go to waste. 'And, in any case, what dog would ever do harm to your grandma, Billy?' she asked.

'I don't know, Grandma.'

'It wouldn't. No dog would. How could it, Billy, after what your grandad did for dogs all his life? Because they know, you know, Billy.

83

Dogs know. They pass it on. They might not be able to talk like us, but they pass it on.'

'How do they do that, Grandma?'

'They leave their trademarks.'

'But how do they pass on their messages?'

'Not even scientists know that, Billy.' I bet they don't! thought Billy. 'Yes,' she said, 'your grandad loved dogs all his life, Billy. In fact, I sometimes think he was fonder of dogs than me . . .'

'Does he still love them?'

'Don't ask silly questions.'

'Has he been to see you again?'

'He's been twice this week.'

'As a ghost, you mean?'

'I wouldn't say that entirely, Billy. I wouldn't go so far as to say that. More like in dreams – in spirit. Personally speaking, like, I can't say I altogether hold with ghosts, though when we lived at Byers Green – that was when your grandad and me was first married – Mrs Petty next door used to see one regular as clockwork every time she went down their cellar to fetch the coals.'

'Did she really?'

'Mr Petty had this habit of keeping his best boots on the cellar steps, and every night in life that ghost used to shift them boots up to the next step.'

'What did it do that for?'

'They never found out, Billy. They even had the Police in about it.'

'Was she frightened?'

'What was there to be frightened of, Our Billy? There's nothing to be frightened of in ghosts. If I opened my wardrobe door tonight and found a ghost standing in there' (Not again! thought Billy. If she mentions that sort of thing just once more tonight I'm emigrating to Australia), 'do you know what I'd do?'

'No,' said Billy. 'What?'

'I'd ask if it was feeling cold, Our Billy. They often do, you know. I'd offer it a blanket. I'd even make it a hot water bottle, if it wanted me to. I'd ask it into bed with us, and give it a cuddle to keep it warm – as long as your grandad had no objections, of course.'

'Ghosts are supposed to haunt you, Grandma.'

'Never in the wide world, Billy. You don't believe everything people tell you. A lot of the stories people tell are nothing but lies.' That was certainly true of some people he knew, thought Billy. 'Shall I tell you what ghosts are, Billy?'

'Yes please,' said Billy.

'They're poor lost souls, more to be pitied than anything else. Some time in their life they've done something they oughtn't to have done, and because of that they have to wait their turn to get into Heaven.'

'You mean they have to sort of queue up? Like for a bus?'

'In a manner of speaking, yes.'

'How long for?'

'Hundreds of years. Sometimes thousands.'

It was no wonder they got cold then, Billy

thought. Even round where Billy lived they didn't have to wait *that* long for the bus.

'That's how I know your grandad isn't one of them. He never did a bad deed in his life. Which is just as well,' Grandma said, 'because he couldn't abide standing in queues, your grandad. He'd rather walk any day than stand in a big queue. But St Peter saw him coming and had the Pearly Gates already wide open for him when he arrived.'

Probably just as well, thought Billy. Walking all the way to heaven would be no mean feat – very punny!

'Has he told you what it's like up there, Grandma?'

'Many a time, pet. He tells us all about it. Sometimes we talk all night after I've given him a cuddle and warmed his feet up – your grandad always had cold feet. You want to ask them next door if they've ever heard us talking.' Here she jabbed the stem of her pipe in the direction of the neighbours. 'Every time they complain about me and your grandad talking, I tell them about that grandson of theirs roaring up the street on his Kassawaki' (she meant Kawasaki) 'like a jet-propelled robot' (she meant rocket). 'That shuts them up!'

'And what's it like in Heaven, Grandma?'

'Bonny, pet. Shiny bits of tinsel hanging down. Plenty to eat and drink, and angels playing music all the time.'

It sounded like the *Blue Room Café* where Billy and his mam sometimes went for a cup of

tea after they'd finished the shopping at Bishop
Auckland. They still hadn't taken the decora-
tions down from last Christmas and you had to
shout your head off to be heard above the
endless belt of muzak.

'And have they got animals up there?'

'Animals? Up in Heaven?' Again she jabbed
with the stem of her pipe, but this time, because
her jab was aimed at Heaven, it was a shade
more gently. 'Any amount of them, Our Billy.
How could you have Heaven without animals?
What a daft question?'

'I was just thinking of – storage space.'

'Storage space? There's any amount of room
up there, Our Billy. You'd know that if your
mother sent you to Sunday School like I've told
her to – not that anybody takes any notice of
me! "In my Father's house are many mansions"
– that's what Our Lord said, and if *He* didn't
know what he was talking about, I'd like to
know who did! Any amount of room. Your grandad's got all the dogs up there he ever had in
life – every single one of them. Our Patch, Our
Betty. Jock, Pegs – we called her that 'cause
she was always pinching the pegs off the line
when we lived down Nelson Street. They're all
there. Do you think your grandad would've
gone to Heaven without his dogs? Not him.
They were inseparable. Like I say, he loved dogs
all his life, your grandad. He's even got that
little pit pony he always wanted in life and
never got.'

'I thought you said last week he never got it?'

87

Chapter 12

Above the bed where Billy slept that night there was a picture of Grandad.

He didn't look very nice. All stiff and solemn looking. He was dressed in a black suit and a white shirt with a stiff collar. The bristles of his moustache were stiff. Everything was.

But the worst thing was the way his eyes followed you about the room, wherever you went. Grandma always said that was a sign of a good picture. It was why she had bought the picture of a poodle at the Church bring and buy sale, the one that was now stuck up on her kitchen wall.

Billy didn't mind so much the poodle watching you all the time while you ate a Digestive biscuit or dried the tea things; but the way Grandad looked at you while you were getting ready for bed was just a bit spooky.

He made sure the window was fastened tight. His grandma was a bit like his mother – a fresh air fiend, always letting what they called 'a breath of fresh air' come into the rooms and freeze you to death.

He did *not* open the wardrobe door.

He was just going to switch off his bedside light when he heard a noise in the passage.

Dot wandered in. They had left her lying by the fire fast asleep and making little snickering noises as she dreamed. She had her golliwog in her mouth. She obviously wanted to get into bed with Billy. And Billy was tempted. But he thought he'd better not.

He ordered her to go back. She looked at him for a second or so, obviously feeling sorry for herself. What an actress she was! Billy had considered going on the telly himself – if Sunderland hadn't signed him on by the time he was sixteen – but if he didn't make it, there was always a good chance that Dot would. He could just imagine her having her own series: *Dotty the Wonder Dog.* She could look really pathetic when she wanted to. He ordered her again. At last she wandered off. She kept looking back over her shoulder to see if he'd changed his mind.

He switched off the light.

He could hear his grandma snoring in the next room. He wondered how far his mam and dad had got by now. Not far. His dad had only been driving for a year, and he was still dead careful. Hands at two o'clock and ten o'clock, eyes straight ahead. Not like Steven, who sometimes drove with one hand hanging out of his window or tapping on the roof. He had a sign in his back window, and when he passed people it lit up and blinked THANK YOU * THANK YOU * THANK YOU * if they'd pulled over to the side.

It would be bad driving in this fog. He could just imagine his dad getting all frazzled. He would be pressed forward against the windscreen. The fog would be rolling up against the glass, all grey, all grey, nothing but grey mist all the way, no time to stay . . .

'Keep your head down, Billy,' said his grandad. 'There's some nasty stones in the roof.'

They were walking down a low dark tunnel. Billy's grandad was still in his stiff dark suit and white collar. The lantern he carried swung from side to side. The walls of the tunnel were shining black and dripping wet.

Billy's grandad stopped. He banged his lantern against the tunnel wall and listened. He'd done that twice before, Billy remembered. When Billy asked him what he was doing, he had just put his finger to his lips as if to say they had to listen.

They walked on.

Billy realized his grandad was now dressed in pit clothes. His face was streaked with grime and sweat. There were dogs all round their feet. Billy knew they'd been there all the time but hadn't noticed them before. His grandad was leading a pit pony and Billy knew its name was Dinky, even though his grandad hadn't told him.

They came to a small chamber cut into the wall. It was a room made of rock. There was a table in it, and a fire was burning in the grate. Two men in olden-day clothes were fighting a duel. A lady in a crinoline was sitting at the table looking sorry. The fighting looked dangerous. One of the suitors was going to get killed. Billy knew.

'I wish they wouldn't do it,' the lady said to Billy. 'All men are daft.'

'Take no notice, Billy, they're only cigarette cards,' said his grandad. 'I know because I collected them.'

The dogs made no sound at all as they walked. Billy knew their paws were wrapped in cotton wool. When he looked, he saw they weren't.

Grandad stopped and knocked on the wall again. This time Billy heard what they were listening for.

Someone was behind the wall. They were digging. They were children. Billy could hear their shovels scraping and now and then the sound of them talking. One little girl was crying.

Billy knew who they were. They were the children of a century ago who had worked down the coalmines. They were only eight years of age. A man in Parliament had spoken up for them. Mrs Drury had told them all about it.

When Billy looked, he saw his grandad had gone on ahead. He had no lantern now, but everything was clear as day. It was just as it had been when the neon light had pinged on in the front room.

They came to another tunnel that joined up from the left. The dogs had gone now. So had the pit pony. They were alone.

Grandad pointed up the new tunnel.

At first Billy saw nothing. Then mist began to float towards him. It wasn't real mist. It was the kind of mist they used on the telly. Elvis said it was called Dry Ice.

There was a shape in the mist. Before Billy could see properly, he knew it was the Ghost Dog. He could see it plainly now. It was very big. It had rough grey hair. Its eyes were blue, but they did not flicker as he expected them to. They were not luminous. It hesitated when it saw Billy.

'You'll have to stroke it,' his grandad said.

The Ghost Dog came towards them. Its blue eyes remained on Billy. It seemed almost afraid of him.

It came on at a slow steady pace.

'You *can't* be frightened of a dog,' said Grandad. 'Not you, Billy.'

Still nearer it came.

Billy was trembling. He wanted to move, but he couldn't.

He felt its cold muzzle touch his hand. He sucked in breath.

His grandad had gone now.

Billy was all alone.

The Ghost Dog began to lick his finger. A big wet tongue licking his fingers, and his face, and his fingers, and—

When he woke, Dot was in bed with him.

He switched on the bedside light. It was four o'clock. He had to be up at seven to catch the bus. Dot's golliwog was on his pillow. He put it back beside her, between her paws, where she liked it. It was all wet and sloppy.

He could hear something from Grandma's room. It sounded like talking. He hoped Gran-

dad was with *her* now.

After he had switched off his light, he lay with his eyes open for a moment. When he was sure he could still hear them talking together, he closed his eyes and fell asleep.

Chapter 13

The sun was trying hard to break through the mist next morning.

Billy caught the bus at the end of Churchfield Road. It was one of Milburn's, an old cronk that just about kept going, like his grandma. Dot sat on the seat beside him, on the window side because she preferred to look out.

Grandma had given him a packed lunch: a pork pie and two sugary doughnuts. Also the bacon rinds from breakfast; but they were a present for the hens.

They passed a woman with a pram as they clanked down the hill, and Billy wondered if that was why his mam and dad had gone to Barnsley – was something up with little Julie?

He got off at Chapel Row and was in the house mixing the hen-mash by twenty past eight. The house seemed empty and hollow-sounding, but he wasn't scared at all now.

In fact, to prove it, Billy went upstairs and looked in all the upstairs rooms. He even looked under all the beds, just for a joke. He noticed his window was open: that must have caused the rustling sound he'd heard last night.

The lady in the crinoline at the top of the stairs was fatter than she'd been in his dream. If she was living nowadays, she'd be on a diet of lentils and skimmed milk, and wearing tight

95

jeans that showed her bum like his sister. Maybe even go jogging.

The sun was definitely spiking through the mist by the time he and Dot were heading up towards the allotments. He was glad she was with him.

In any case, there was no sign of the Ghost Dog in the allotment. There were no dead hens. There were no large pawprints in the soil round the Brussels sprouts. He looked to see.

He let out the pigeons, then the hens. He was giving the hens the bacon rinds when he heard voices beyond the hawthorns at the top of their allotment. They sounded far away. He wondered vaguely whose they were.

It wasn't until after he'd gathered the eggs and shut the run gate behind him that he went through the hawthorn hedge to look.

The mist was clearing fast now. Two men were striding along the Old Line, one of them taking big strides to match the sleepers that were all that remained of the railway track that had once carried coal trucks from Shilton Colliery.

Billy knew both men. The one taking giant steps was Elvis's uncle, Dasher Potter. The other was Tommy Harle. Both men had their dogs with them, Mr Harle's mucky-grey lurcher stalking ahead of them, and Dasher Potter's terriers scurrying at their heels. And both men had shotguns, broken over their arms. They were heading towards Foxcover Wood and beyond that the motorway, from which Billy

96

could hear the hum of traffic, hidden even now by the mists.

Then he noticed more men. Eight or nine of them, one of them wearing what could have been a policeman's uniform. They were moving slowly along the top of the limestone quarry on the opposite side of the valley. They had sticks and were beating the bushes as they went. From time to time they called down to the two men on the Old Line below.

Then Billy noticed something that made his heart bound.

It was Dot. She was twenty yards off to his right, not far from where he had found her the previous evening. She was moving forward slowly, her daft tail stuck up in the air, her head poked forward.

'Come here!' he called, as loudly as he dared.

He didn't dare call any louder. If he attracted the attention of the two gunmen, they might easily look up and see her. And at that range, half-seeing her sliding along the hedge part-hidden by tall yellow grass and giant hogweed, they might easily mistake her for something else.

He called her again.

Of course, she took no notice.

Billy crouched down as low as he could and began running along the hedge towards her. When one of the men on the quarry top called out, he fell flat on the wet grass, fearing a shot. But none came.

'Dot! Here!' He was frightened to death the

men would see her.

She took no notice.

Billy crawled towards her.

She was acting in a really funny way. Her nose was pointed at the hedge. Her body was all low and stretched out, her head was practically on the ground.

'Come here, you stupid animal!'

When he tried to grab her she circled to her

left, away from him, her nose still pointing at
the same spot, as if drawn by a magnetic force.

'Come here!'

She wouldn't leave.

But Billy couldn't take any chances. He lunged
out to his left and caught hold of her collar. She
struggled to pull away but he dug his heels in.
It was a hard job pulling her and his sleeve got
caught in the hawthorn.

As he pulled himself free, the hawthorn
shook. A cloud of black flies buzzed out from
inside it and, at the same time, a terrible thick
smell made him catch his breath. It was so
awful that for a moment he almost let go of
Dot's collar.

Then he gritted his teeth and began to pull
away. It wasn't easy. She made it as awkward
as she could. She kept struggling to get back.
He had to force and drag her every inch of the
way through the hedge and the allotment. He
didn't feel safe till he had her outside the
allotment gate with her lead on.

It wasn't until he was halfway down the path
through the allotments that he realized he had
forgotten the eggs.

Chapter 14

And it wasn't till he shut the gate behind him at the very bottom of the allotments that he remembered what the smell from the bush was.

It was the smell of something dead.

A few months back they'd all noticed this sickly smell in their kitchen, a smell that every day grew sweeter and stronger and more sickly.

His mam had looked everywhere. She'd had the fridge dragged out. Completely emptied the cupboards. Even had the floorboards taken up.

It was only when his dad took the front off the control panel on the gas oven that they discovered the cause. A mouse had been electrocuted to death when it trod on one of the electric wires. Billy's dad said someone must have pressed the ignition switch at precisely the moment when the mouse was clambering over the electric wires – a chance in a thousand, he said.

There was something dead under that bush. It wasn't only the smell. It was the flies as well.

At first, Billy had thought it might be the Ghost Dog up there. But it couldn't have been. It had enough opportunity to attack him when he was rolling about trying to control daft Dotty, if it had wanted to. But there'd been no growl, no nothing.

He'd have a look tonight when he went up to feed the hens. Lucky his mam and dad were away, really. Otherwise, his dad might have been real sarky about the eggs.

But, in fact, his mam and dad were back already when he got home. He saw them the moment he pushed open the yard gate: they were both standing by the kitchen table, looking out through the window, as if there was something to see.

Before he had barely set foot in the house his dad said to him quietly, 'Your sister and the bairn's come up with us.' He nodded his head in the direction of the other room, from where, to Billy's surprise, he could hear the telly on already. Normally his mam and dad considered it a mortal sin to watch the telly before the evening news – unless, of course, there was international snooker or football on, and then things were different. 'So just watch what you say when you go in there.'

'Isn't Steven with them?'

He almost whispered the words. It was likely that he should never have uttered them at all, but they'd sort of slipped out: it seemed so – wrong – Steven not being there. Unnatural.

His dad glanced quickly at his mother before he spoke, and then said only the one word:

'No.'

'You'd best go and say hello to them,' his mam said. 'But you haven't all day.'

His sister and little Julie were sitting on the sofa gawping at the telly. They were still in their hats and coats, as if they didn't intend stopping five minutes: but there were two hefty suitcases

plonked along the back of the sofa. Julie had a
biscuit in her hand, which she wasn't eating, and
a man in a green velvet jacket on breakfast telly
was describing in glowing terms the high protein
value of kidney beans; but neither Sandra or Julie
were really listening.

'What you doing here, Our Sandra?' asked
Billy. He meant it to be funny, light-hearted, but
realized at once that it wasn't.

'Mind, that's a nice welcome!' Sandra said,
trying to smile, but not quite managing. 'How you
getting on, Our Billy?'

'Champion. How are you?'

Looking down at her he could see the streaks
where she'd been crying, and her face looked
drawn and pale.

'Not so bad.'

She looked away.

'And how's that cheeky little girl?' Billy asked.
Normally Julie liked being called cheeky. But she
made no response now, except to put her thumb
in her mouth. Anybody would have thought she
was really interested in what Mr Velvet Jacket
was saying about Brussels sprouts and fresh
spinach. 'Has the cat got your tongue, little Miss
Cheeky?'

'She's maybe a bit tired,' said Sandra.

She likely would be. They would all be tired.
But it wasn't just that, Billy thought.

'Billy!'

That was his mam calling him from the
kitchen.

'Right,' said Billy talking to the back of Julie's

102

head, 'I'll come and grab a kiss from the lovely girl before I go to school. A right smackeroodle!'

'Billy!'

When he went back into the kitchen, his dad said, 'Your mam doesn't want you saying overmuch, Billy. Your sister'll not take a lot of upsetting, not this morning.'

'I'm not daft, you know,' Billy said to his mam.

'Nobody ever said you were,' his dad said. 'And there's no need to use that kind of language to your mother.'

'When's Steven coming?' Billy asked. He tried to keep his voice down well below the level of the telly and at the same time let them know quite clearly he was narked – because he *was* narked. He felt that in some inexplicable way Mrs Potter had known more about what was really going on than he knew even now.

'Mebbies later on,' his mam said. The kettle boiled and she took the teapot over to it to scald the tea. 'We can't say for sure, really. You can leave this rubbish here,' she said pointing to the packed lunch his grandma had made him. 'The hens'll eat it. You get a proper dinner, as usual.'

'What the devil's got into that dog this morning?' his dad said.

It was true that Dot hadn't stopped nithering and whining at the back door since she'd come in, but Billy knew he was only trying to distract him from asking awkward questions. His dad was all for the calm life.

'There's something up in the hedge, Dad, behind Mr Haddall's.'

'Like what?'
'Something dead, I think.'
'What for you didn't look, Our Billy?'
'There were some fellars down on the Old Line.

Elvis's uncle and Mr Harle. They had guns, both of them.'

'Shoot first, and ask later – that's their motto!'

'Let that dog out, Dick, she's getting on my nerves,' said Billy's mam.

'Me and Billy'll get some coal.'

As Billy and his dad stepped out into the yard, Dot shot through his dad's legs and nearly upscuttled him, so that he came out with a really flowery mouthful. She ran straight to the back gate and started leaping up at it.

'The animal's gone crackers!'

'I had a heck of a job dragging her away, Dad.'

'I'll mebbies have a look up there later on. Like as not, it'll be a rabbit or summat. It'll be neither nowt nor summat when it's all there.'

'And I forgot the eggs, Dad.'

Billy had opened the coalhouse door now, and had started to fill the coal bucket.

'You never did, Billy? That's not like you. Look at the daft thing jumping up and down like a yoyo!' He came over to Billy. 'Son, if I were you I wouldn't mention Steven for a day or two, like. Just till things blow over.'

'What's he done, Dad?'

'Storm in a teacup, Billy.'

That was a fat lot of good. That really made things clear.

'But what's he done, though?'

'Least said, soonest mended in these matters, Billy,' his dad said.

Billy had finished filling the coal. He closed the door and dropped the bent nail in the hasp. He picked up the coal bucket in one hand and the fire shovel in the other.

'And, Billy –'

'Yes, Dad?'

'Just watch what you say when you go back in there, won't you, son? We don't want Our Sandra and that bairn upsetting any more.'

Billy said nothing. What he would have liked to have done was given his dad a proper one on the napper with the coal shovel.

Chapter 15

If Elvis hadn't decided to chuck the stinkbomb that day, and Billy hadn't decided to wait for him after school, things would probably have turned out slightly different that weekend.

Elvis's mother was too humane to force him to eat what was commonly referred to as 'school sludge', so he was able to lob his stinkbomb through the open window of the girls' indoor toilet just as the second-sitting victims – which included Mrs Drury's class – were preparing for an onslaught of semolina pud doled in their direction by Mrs Ward – Emma's mother – and her well-drilled army of no-nonsense serving ladies.

A second after Elvis had perpetrated his evil deed, he ran straight into the welcoming arms of Mr Fixby, who hugged him warmly to his manly chest for a moment, before picking him up by the seat of his raggy pants and bearing him proudly aloft like a hunting trophy in the direction of Mr Starr's office.

But by then the damage was done. Just as Billy was spooning as much blackcurrant jam as a spoon could possibly spoon onto his semolina pud (you needed a lot of jam to drown the taste) the first all-but-gassed girls ran screaming from the bomb-ravaged toilets and fled down the corridors, followed on their heels by the

107

Elvis

deadly poisonous pong that had soon insinuated itself into every dusty corner of the school, including the dining hall.

It was a smell so thick that it would have been possible to walk on it. If someone had stood the smell up on its side, they could have wall-papered it. A smell of definitely rotten eggs. Highly concentrated definitely rotten eggs. Rotten eggs *par excellence*.

Mrs Ward – always a practical woman – immediately slammed down the corrugated metal blinds over her serving hatch, thus preserving from further harm the leftovers of semolina pud, herself, and her trusty bank of strong-armed supporters.

It would be like this when the Bomb went off, Billy had often thought. A lot of handy shutters slamming down all round him – and he wouldn't be safely behind any of them. At the same time, there'd be an awful lot of chaos and confusion: just as there was now.

They'd just got new seats in the dining hall. Mr Starr had called them a 'breakthrough in canteen furniture design': four cups of plastic (moulded to fit four little bums) all joined together with a long metal pole. They were a good idea as far as stacking was concerned: they took less time to clear away and less space when they were.

But they did have a drawback. Because they were so light they did have a tendency to fall over – just about all the time. And when they did fall over they did it with a clatter. And that is precisely what happened when the pong of exceedingly rotten eggs began poking itself up the noses of the diners, and then diving down their throats.

It was just like a film Billy had seen on the telly last Christmas. Mr Starr was shouting 'Everyone keep calm! I order everyone to keep calm!' and at the far end of the hall Mrs Dill was screaming 'Evacuate! Evacuate!' like a Dalek in a red trouser suit.

If the War had still been on, Mrs Wendover would have got a medal because she just stood there gathering her Infants about her like a broody mother hen, clucking away composedly all the while and gathering them within the voluminous folds of her skirt – which looked to be constructed of two striped Mexican blankets, outsize.

Two little kids on the table next to Billy's started shouting 'Gas attack!' and one clutched his throat and said 'Aaargh!' and whopped his head down on the table, narrowly missing death in the form of a plate of semolina pud. A lot followed his example, as you might expect.

It was really great. As Billy filed out to the relative safety of the playground, he had to step over a girl called Deborah Parret who was rolling on the floor and clutching her stomach and saying she was dying. Deborah Parret was always rolling on the floor and saying she was dying. She had a terrible imagination.

The last thing Billy saw, as he went through the french window into the yard, was Mrs Drury

110

conducting a full-scale search in her handbag
and he guessed that could only mean one thing:
her migraine had swooped back into attack.

Mrs Drury was often swooped on by her
migraines, and especially on Friday afternoons,
which coincidentally, were often the times Elvis
reached a climax of mischief and naughtiness.
In fact, she had lately had so many Friday
afternoon attacks that last week Elvis had
asked if they should include it on their time-
tables.

It usually meant they spent the last two hours
of school that week playing Three of a Kind or
doing crosswords that Samantha Soskiss copied
on the blackboard while Mrs Drury attended to
her knitting, which seemed to have a thera-
peutic effect.

And normally Billy wouldn't have minded so
much, because as long as you gave Mrs Drury a
more or less quiet life during one of her migraine attacks you could more or less get up to
what you liked, providing you did it reasonably
quietly. It was only if you made her drop one of
her loops that she threw one of her nasty hairy
tempers.

But this Friday was different. Ever since the
Ghost Dog had surfaced into the news she had
been reading them extracts from *The Hound of
the Baskervilles*, and she was just coming up to
the really exciting bit.

But, as it turned out, she did read the story
after all – though for a worryingly long time it
looked as if she wouldn't. The migraine per-

sisted until afternoon break, but just after break it miraculously cleared up. Perhaps the news that Elvis had to report to Mr Starr's office for the cane and then spend the rest of the afternoon waiting outside his office had something to do with the amazing recovery.

A little tremor of excitement ran through the class as she delicately lowered her specs onto her sensitive ears and tentatively picked up the book. Crosswords on the very point of completion were callously abandoned and put finally to rest in desks whose lids were lowered with the concerned silence of visitors to a sick bed in hospital.

Only when all the sniffs at hankies and scuffs of feet had stopped did Mrs Drury begin.

She was, in fact, a very good reader. It was only a pity she didn't read more often. In fact, it is a mark of her overwhelming excellence that even Elvis – of all people – had once been heard to whisper 'Skill!' reverently during her rendering of what he still regarded as one of the all-time greats of English Literature: a story about giant snails that devoured a brainy teacher alive, a story which, as you might expect, appealed to his natural sense of justice.

She really was ace, Billy was thinking. You could see she wasn't a member of St Luke's Hammerchewers for nothing. She could put on all the different accents and could even make her face change to suit the part.

When she was Sherlock Bones, as Elvis called him, her voice went as sharp as vinegar, and when she was hot on the scent of a clue her nose seemed to extend and almost quiver. When she was poor, daft Dr Watson, her face sort-of rounded-out and started looking as healthy as a russet apple; at the same time her mouth wobbled as she spoke and appeared to be crammed full of soggy walnuts and chewed-off bits of moustache whisker.

And the whole time she was on the move: strolling restlessly back and forth in front of her desk or darting down the aisles like a Ferret scout-car, spinning round on her heel in shock, or suddenly staggering backwards in surprise and nearly upending herself in the wastepaper basket.

At the same time she threw in a more than liberal supply of gestures to indicate the gist of the story to those that were too dim to follow it otherwise.

Sometimes she stared at the back of the wall until her eyes almost popped out of their sockets and Pat Shufflebotham started whimpering. Or the hand that wasn't holding the book would creep quiveringly up to her throat and then, quite often, attempt to throttle her, again causing the eyes to bulge and Pat Shufflebotham to whimper.

At other times she would throw the same spare hand up in the air with shock, horror, or amazement – maybe all three at once. Or she would collapse like a sack of depressed taties into her teacher's chair and twice as suddenly leap out of it six feet out of the air, as if she'd just sat on the sharpened point of one of her own monster-sized knitting needles.

Just before afternoon school ended, she reached the part where poor Dr Watson was out on the moor alone, fumbling and bumbling his way about with no idea of what was happening, either in the story or in the mists all round him. The dark was closing in like a murderous enemy, and the hound had already slipped from its chain and was closing fast.

Mrs Drury kept losing her footing and stumbling over the unpredictable ground beneath her high-heeled shoes, and once she leaned over too far and clonked Alison Fretwell on the napper – but like the experienced old trouper she was she coolly ignored it. She was just looking over her shoulder, her eyes (once again) popping, as she listened to a sinister sound over by the book cupboard when the bell rang – and the whole class nearly jumped out of their skins.

The whole class except Billy, that is.

Two paragraphs back his mind had somehow started wandering off towards his sister and Steven and little Julie. Perhaps it was because like poor Dr Watson they seemed to Billy so stumbling and bumbling, so confused, and, at least for the moment, so lost in a fog.

'What on earth are you dreaming about now, Robinson?'

'Nothing, miss. I was listening.'

'What were the last words I spoke?'

Pause. 'Miss, was it "Dr Watson"?'

'Rubbish! You can stay behind after school,

Robinson, and pick up every piece of litter from this floor! Every piece! And you'll stay in until it's tidy!'

Chapter 16

By the time Mrs Drury had condescended to let him go it was five past four, and as Billy went into the entrance lobby he saw that Elvis was still standing there outside Mr Starr's office.

'How long you got to stop there?'

'Mr Starr sez till quarter past.'

'How many did he give you?'

'Couple on each mitt.'

Elvis showed his hands. The white marks were still visible. Up till that point Billy had still been sorry for himself.

'Did it hurt much?'

'Na.'

'I'll wait for you,' said Billy.

He pretended to be looking at the road safety exhibition done by the top class when Mr Starr came out to dismiss Elvis.

'Off you go now, Elvis, and no more stink-bombs – you hear me?'

'Sir.'

'And what are you hanging about for, Robinson? Not waiting around for this reprobate, are you?'

'No, sir. Just looking at this display.'

'Didn't know you were so keen on road safety. You wouldn't like to write me an essay on it over the weekend?'

'No, sir.'

'Thought not,' said Mr Starr, bobbing back into his office with a sly smile on his face. He could still crack a corny joke now and again.

As they walked along Station Road, cars were already beginning to put on their sidelights. At the corner of Chapel Row they saw Pat Shufflebotham and Little Chuff waiting for their mam and dad to come back from somewhere – they were always locking them out. Little Chuff was crying because somebody had ripped the strap off his Amazing Spiderman bag, and his sister had that awful faraway look in her eyes.

The first thing Billy saw when he went in their backyard was Dot tied to the downpipe from the roof gutter. He could see that she'd pulled over the dustbin because there was still a bit of mess left. His dad must have tidied up: if it had been his mam there wouldn't have been a sign of muck left.

'Mind, you're late back,' his mam said, as he stepped into the kitchen. 'Wherever have you been till this time of night?'

'Stopped behind to wait for Elvis.' He didn't bother to mention the Keep Britain Tidy bit with Mrs Drury: his mam tended to go stark raving mad bonkers if he got into the slightest bit of bother at school. He slung his bag on the floor and sat down at the table.

'And what's Elvis been up to now?' asked his dad, coming in from the other room and looking, Billy thought, rather pleased with himself for some reason. 'Not been seeing that dog again, has he?'

117

'Let a stinkbomb off in the girls' lavvy.'

Billy screwed off the top of the pop bottle and poured himself a drink.

'And you stopped behind and walked back with him?' his mam said. 'After all that, Our Billy?'

'All what?'

'I've told you! Watch your tongue, young man, when you talk to your mother!'

Watching the fizz rising up in his drink reminded Billy of the fizz that was rising up in his brain just at the moment.

'You never told him anything?'

'What about, Mam?'

'You know very well what about. Our Sandra.'

'No.'

'Are you sure?'

Did they think he was a liar or something? Was that it? It was true he had *considered* telling Elvis, just to get his own back, but in the end he hadn't.

'He didn't winkle it out of you?' his mam continued.

'He never even tried, Mam.'

'It's a wonder! I know what them Potters are like!'

'Me and your mother can't reckon up what you see in the lad, Billy.'

The point was, they never liked anybody he ever went around with. One freezing cold day last winter he'd gone in Emma Ward's house for five minutes and eaten a hot mince pie, and his

118

mother had played heck about it for months after. She said that Mrs Ward was a stuck-up snob who wouldn't hang her washing out the fronts like everybody else in the street, and that he never ate her own mince pies. Which was true: but Mrs Ward's mince pies tasted different.

'The Potters are the lowest of the low,' his mam said.

That was it, thought Billy. The mams and dads of the kids he went about with were either stuck-up snobs or the lowest of the low. They had to be one or the other.

'What is it about the lad you like?'

'He's just my best pal, Dad.'

'Is he?'

'Yes.' He spoke almost defiantly.

'Just so long as we know,' his dad said.

There was an uneasy silence after that. There was no sound from the other room, so he guessed his sister and Julie must have gone out for a breath of fresh air. He remembered the time when they'd yackered on at his sister like this, before she'd got married. Once when they'd been going on about some disco she wanted to go to, she had accidentally knocked his dad's pipe out of his mouth and it had broken when it hit the fireplace. Sandra had been really upset by that, and had rushed upstairs crying and wouldn't come out of her room for hours. Even when they begged her to go to the disco she'd refused to come out. She was like that. But he knew how she felt. One of these days they'd drive *him* to marriage!

Eventually, when Billy had composed himself and finished his two slices of jam and bread, he said, to clear the air:

'Did you have a look up in the hedge, Dad?'

There might have been a slight pause before his dad spoke.

'I did.' He lit his pipe and put the burnt match back in his box. 'Just a rabbit.'

'What did you do with it?'

'Threw it over the Edge.'

Billy pushed back his chair and got up.

'You can tidy that bag away, young man, before you do anything else,' his mam said. 'Get it up to your room, where it belongs.'

'Can I do it after I've fed the hens, Mam?'

'I'll see to the hens meself tonight, son,' his dad said.

'What for, Dad?'

His mam said, 'You'll still get your pocket money, Billy, won't he, Dick?'

'Course the lad will. No question at all about that.'

Billy didn't know what to say. For over a year now Billy had seen to the hens and pigeons himself at teatime. It was his job.

'It's just that that dog's been on the loose round here, hasn't it Dick?'

'That's right. They reckon it's broke into a fellar's hut down Crag End way and killed a dozen banties.'

'It could've been a fox, Dad.'

'It wasn't a fox.'

'A fox would've polished the lot off, wouldn't it, Dick?'

'That's right. A fox would've done the lot in. So I don't want you going up that allotment for the next few days. Have you got that?'

'Yes, Dad.'

'And you can stop in tonight,' his mam said. 'We don't want you going round to the Potters' again, not for a few days.'

'Can't I go out somewhere else, Mam?'

'No. You can get up in your room and do some tidying up,' she said. 'Just for a change.'

Chapter 17

The next morning, Saturday, Butch held his war party meeting in their den in the abandoned tunnel that years ago had been driven into the face of the limestone quarry.

They were twenty feet in, shielded from the outside world by boulders that had fallen from the roof before any of them had been born. Close by was a pool of water that was constantly fed from drips on the roof. Because of this water Butch reckoned they would be able to last out forever if the Crag Enders' gang ever tried to besiege them. He was nuts.

Up to fifty feet in, the tunnel walls and roof were lined with bricks that were always dripping wet and slimed-over with green weed. Further in there was just bare stone. As far as anyone had explored, there were junction boxes for electricity all the way along the walls, but they had never been wired up.

Nobody knew how far the tunnel went in because nobody had ever reached the end. Fifty yards in, it became pitch black. A torch only seemed to make matters worse, because when you switched it on the darkness around you seemed to thicken up and close in around you. When you looked back at the entrance it was only a tiny speck of light.

A hundred yards in, the floor fell away beneath your feet. Down in the bottom you had to scramble over boulders that felt to be the size of large cars. If you missed your footing you fell into pools that were full of icy water and very deep. The slightest sound you made echoed and boomed. You could *feel* the darkness pressing into your face like cold, black, flannel.

Nobody had got any further than this. Not even Elvis.

Butch wasn't just nuts this morning. This morning he was *particularly* nuts. That was because he and Elvis had just discovered that the Gang's lookout post up in Foxcover Wood had been wrecked by the Crag Enders.

'How do we know it was them?' Billy had asked.

'Who else would it be, dumbbell?'

Butch glared at him over the top of the crate that was their conference table.

'Could've been the CIA!' suggested Elvis.

'Shut your cakehole, Elvis!'

'Or mebbies the Russians?'

'I've warned you!'

Elvis took a lot of shutting up.

Little Chuff giggled.

'And you can shut up an' all, Chuffy!'

After that Butch had picked the war party that was going to smash the Crag Enders' camp to smithereens and little pieces: Elvis, Sneck, Ibbo, Daz, and Little Chuff were to come with him.

'What about me?' said Billy.

Butch

'You and Joey can go up to Foxcover and repair the lookout,' Butch said.

'Why can't I come with the rest of you?' asked Billy.

He was always having to go with Joey nowadays. That was because Joey was good at Art and didn't like fighting: Butch was always trying to make Billy look a softy. 'Because I say so!' Butch shouted. 'You can take Wardy and all – if you like!'

Emma was always trying to join their gang. Billy had seen her waiting outside, just where the quarry opened onto the Old Line.

'You'd better tek some ropes to haul things back up,' said Elvis, and he came over to help Billy find a good one.

'Best to keep your trap shut when Bonzo the Mad Bear's around!' Elvis said to Billy, nodding back at Butch.

'I'm sick of him!' said Billy.

'Hurry up, Elvis!' Butch shouted over to him.

'Yes, bwana! Yes, Big White God! Coming right away, Big Chief Sitting-bum!' He went over to Butch, grovelling all the time like somebody in a pantomime.

Emma Ward was still where Billy had seen her ten minutes before, standing in one of the lime kilns at the quarry opening. In the old days the kilns, which were like very large brick-lined ovens with no front, had been used to burn lime. They always reminded Billy of the sort of niches where the Ancient Egyptians used to put the statues of their gods and goddesses.

Emma looked down at them as they passed below her.

'Where you off, Billy?'

'Nowhere.'

'Can I come with you?'

Neither Billy nor Joey answered her.

They heard her jump down and start to follow them.

The metal tracks of the Old Line had long since been taken away and the sleepers were sunk deep into the earth and half-covered by pineapple weed and tufts of grass. They were halfway to Foxcover Wood before Joey turned round and said:

'Why you keep following us, Wardy?'

'Because I want to.'

'The Crag Enders might be up there.'

'I'm not scared of them!'

'Let her come,' said Billy.

Foxcover Wood was five minutes walk along the Old Line, on the left-hand side. The cart track from Morgan's farm ran down the west side of the wood before cutting across the Old Line. It was down this cart track that the Crag Enders often came on their raiding parties.

Mr Morgan was going to chop down Foxcover Wood. The EEC was giving him a grant to do it. It was nothing but a bunch of old trees, anyhow: mainly oak and beech. It was all right for getting holly berries and blackberries, and people caught rabbits there. But Mrs Drury referred to it as 'a priceless heritage' and she was getting up a campaign to save it. She was always getting het-up about something or other.

Funnily enough, Billy's grandma didn't want Foxcover to go, either; and she hated the Drurys like condensed poison. Mrs Drury had got her chucked off the flower-arranging committee at St Luke's and every time Mr Drury, who played the organ at St Luke's, passed her in the street he had to avoid using her name because he could never remember it. 'Because the likes of me isn't good enough for the likes of them!' Grandma had said. She would have signed the protest form, only Mrs Drury's name was at the top of it.

The Crag Enders had completely wrecked the lookout post.

The boards and mats that had been the flooring were strewn around in the bracken. They had pinched the corrugated iron sheet which had been the roof. They had even tried to bend the six-inch nails that were nailed in the trunk to climb up with.

Billy, Joey, and Emma gathered up everything first, then Billy climbed up to where the trunk branched out and secured the rope at one end and lowered the other down so that Joey and Emma could pass things up.

It took a long time. Wedging the planks in was hard.

A squirrel came to watch them. At first it was scared, but after a bit it sneaked closer. Eventually it came so far down it was level with Billy, about twenty feet above ground. It was really inquisitive.

They were all up in the lookout having a rest after covering the floor with bracken – that was Emma's idea – when they heard voices.

It was two men with shotguns.

They fired almost immediately. They couldn't have seen Billy, Joey, and Emma, because they'd flattened themselves onto the floor.

They heard a thump.

When they lifted their heads to look, they saw the squirrel on the ground. It was dead. One of the men kicked it as he passed.

Billy didn't speak. Neither did Joey or Emma. They didn't even go to look at the squirrel, let alone bury it.

What was so terrible was the sudden easy way in which it had died.

Chapter 18

Billy decided to say nothing about what had happened when he got home. If his mam and dad knew somebody was taking potshots at him they would have kept him locked up in the house for thirty years: he'd have been like the Man in the Iron Mask.

Personally, he hadn't been too worried hearing the shot whistling past his ears. It was the killing of the squirrel that had upset him. The way it had been alive and interested one minute and stone dead the next. That was what had shocked him. Shocked the others, as well. They'd none of them spoke hardly a word all the way back along the Old Line. They hadn't gone to look at it, either, before they came away, let alone give the thing a decent burial.

There was a horrible pong from something cooking in a big pan on the stove and at first he thought it was for his dinner. He was somewhat relieved when his mam said it was dog food but he did feel sorry for Dot: there *was* an awful lot of it. As if she didn't have enough to bear already. She was still tied up to the drainpipe, still dithering and whining on.

Grandma came down just before twelve – she usually managed to land about mealtimes, just by coincidence of course.

She was dressed in a pair of furry green and

orange moon boots and a grey fur coat that Billy hadn't seen before.

'What do you reckon to these, Our Alice?' she said, twirling round. 'How much do you think these cost me?'

'Twenty pence, Mother?'

'What do you mean?'

'Haven't you just got them at a jumble sale?'

'Ten pence for the coat, and twenty for the boots.'

'I thought as much!'

'Does it look like that?'

'You look an absolute sight, Mother!'

'Well, I thought I looked really smart.'

'You haven't come down in the bus like that!'

'Well, I haven't flown down,' said Grandma. She took off her gloves and put them on the kitchen table. 'Where's Our Sandra, then? I suppose I better have a word with her.'

'Just watch what you say, Mother.'

'I wasn't born yesterday, you know, Alice!'

Billy followed his grandma into the other room. Sandra was apparently watching a cartoon on the telly. Julie was on her knee, her thumb jammed in her mouth where it had been more or less since she'd come.

'Looks like you're dressed for the Arctic!' Billy's dad said to Grandma.

'It's just a bit chilly in here,' said Grandma. She always said that when she was narked. It wasn't cold at all. With the fire blazing away and the oven as well, it was like a hothouse. She ensconced herself in the comfy chair near the

131

telly. 'Mind, this is a fine carry-on, Our Sandra,' she said.

'Hello, Grandma,' said Sandra, hardly taking her eyes off the cartoon.

'And when do you intend to go back to him?'

'She says she isn't going back, Mother,' said Billy's mam who had wandered in from the kitchen. 'That's what she reckons at present.'

'Well, I've never heard of anything so crackers in all my life!' said Grandma.

'Don't you start, Gran,' said Sandra. She kept her eyes locked on to the cartoon. A cat was sharpening up an axe and at the same time a mouse was painting the end of the cat's tail to look like a mouse. 'I've made up my mind, and that's final!'

Adults were daft sometimes, Billy thought. It was easy to see that Sandra would go back to Steven as it was to see what the cat was going to swipe at with its sharpened axe in two seconds. They'd been married for three years now, and they still went gooey when they clapped eyes on one another. Steven even kissed her before he went to work.

'And have you thought about that little bairn?' asked Grandma, unloosening the buttons of her ten pence fur coat because she was starting to boil already. 'What about that little lass?'

'It's because of her that I've come up here in the first place, Gran!' Sandra snapped. Her eyes flashed at the same time. Although she was little and skinny, Billy's sister had always had

132

the knack of going off like a firecracker when she wanted to. And it was best to be out of her way when she ignited. 'I don't want any advice, thank you!'

The cat cut off the end of its own tail and went through the ceiling like a rocket.

'Keep your shirt on, lass,' said Billy's dad.

Did he *really* think girls wore shirts?

'Well, all I can say is I'm grateful your grandfather isn't alive to see this day,' said Grandma. 'He'd be ashamed! Ashamed!'

'Oh, Mother, let the matter drop now,' said Billy's mam.

'Quite right,' said Billy's dad. 'We don't want no words. Not at a time like this. We don't want to get aeriated.'

'Your father and me never had a carry-on like this, Our Alice,' said Grandma. 'Fifty years we were married and we never had a cross word.'

'What baloney, Mother! You were always rowing!'

'Alice! I don't know how you can stand there in front of me and say such a thing! We never had an angry word all our lives!'

'Mother! You and dad were always having words, you know you were! You were like cat and dog sometimes.'

'I'm not going to stand here and be insulted like this by my own daughter,' said Grandma, who was still sitting down.

'You want to take that coat off,' said Billy's dad. 'You're starting to look like an overheated lobster.'

'All I'm saying, Mother, is that all couples have their ups and downs,' said Billy's mam.

'Not me and your father, Alice. Never. Not to my memory.'

'Just shut up the pair of you,' said Billy's dad. 'This sort of talk's not going to mend matters, is it? And that's all we want – this matter mending.'

'I'm not going back to him, Dad,' said Sandra, 'if that's what you mean!'

'Nobody said you had to, lass.'

'As long as that's understood.'

'I'm sure we never once had words,' Grandma was saying, as she extricated herself from her fur coat. 'Not once.' She started to unzip her moon boots. 'I could do with a cup of tea if there is one, Alice.'

'The dinner'll be ready in five minutes, Mother. I expect you'll be stopping for a bite to eat?'

'Just as long as I'm welcome, Alice. I don't want to stop where I'm not wanted.'

Billy's mam gathered up her coat and tam-o'-shanter and went to hang them up. On the telly the cat was just lighting a long fuse tied to a bomb, not realizing that the mouse had just placed the bomb tied to the end of it under the cat's tail.

'Fancy a fill of baccy?' Billy's dad said, handing across his pouch to Grandma.

As his dad's hand moved through the air, Billy caught the faintest whiff of something. Not tobacco. Something else. It was a smell he

134

knew well, not unpleasant, a bit on the sweet side. For some strange reason it reminded him of Steven. Had he smelled it when Steven had been in hospital with a broken leg?

'I'll not say no,' said Grandma. She rummaged in her handbag and eventually dug out a pipe – not the one that had been Grandad's – but another, one with a remarkably large bowl, the one she always took out visiting which she called her 'begging bowl'.

She shovelled in about half the contents of Billy's dad's pouch and then asked him for a match as she handed back the pouch of baccy – or what was left of it. His dad passed over his matches.

Again the mysterious scent teased Billy's nostrils.

'Like I say, Dick,' said Grandma, getting up steam, 'it's just that bit bairn I'm worried about, and in my opinion—'

That was as far as she got.

Sandra burst into tears. She ran upstairs, slamming the passage door behind her.

Julie continued to stare at the telly, her thumb still stuck in her mouth: when the bomb went off under the cat's tail, she scarcely blinked.

Chapter 19

That was how it was all Saturday afternoon. To make matters worse, the mist settled over them again, making the house seem shut in with gloom.

When Billy went out at three o'clock, Sandra was still crying, his grandma was still going on about how perfectly happy she'd been all her life with Grandad, and Dot was still whining to be out at the backdoor. His mam was in the kitchen making gingerbread men with little Julie, her tears plop-plopping onto the pastry.

Joey wasn't allowed out and Billy couldn't find another soul to play with. The streets were deserted. He guessed the war party was still down in Doggy Wood, wrecking dens or burning rope – or something equally nutty. He was glad he wasn't with them. And sorry.

He went down to the Old Line with only the vague notion of what he was going to do, and started walking along it. He wasn't surprised to see Emma by the quarry entrance. She waited for him to catch up.

'Where is everybody?' he asked her.

She shrugged her shoulders. 'What are you going to do, Billy?'

'Don't know.'

'Are you going to bury that squirrel?'

'I was thinking of it.'

'I'll come with you.'

They found it in the bracken where the man had kicked it. They dug a hole with a stick and a stone. They put the squirrel in and covered it with stones, then put the turf back. Emma dragged over a big stone to put on the top.

'It might stop that Ghost Dog getting it,' she said.

'Are you scared of it?' asked Billy.

'Not when you're here, Billy,' she said. 'Are you?'

'I was at first,' Billy admitted, 'but not now.'

Billy led the way as they went back. He took them across the Old Line first. Then they scrambled up the Edge where it was only a few feet high and began to walk along it.

He made sure Emma kept a few feet behind him, just in case. And when he reached the big hawthorn at the back of Mr Haddall's allotment, he told Emma to stay back till he called her.

But it was just as he thought. Whatever it was that had been under the hawthorn had gone now. Perhaps – as his dad reckoned – it had been only a dead rabbit? Perhaps.

He looked hard into the darkness under the bush for several seconds, but there was nothing to see. Not even any black flies when he shook the branches on purpose. Even the awful smell had gone, or almost. Just a faint suggestion of it hung on the air.

There *was* another smell, however. One that he had already come across not two hours before in the house – the one on his dad's hands. He didn't understand at first.

He waved Emma to come forward.

'What's that smell?' he asked her.

She knew straight off.

'TCP.'

Of course! That was it! Or Tom Cat's Pittle, as Steven always called it.

He smiled. He was beginning to understand

what was going on.

He smiled even more when they noticed the wide looping swathe in the grass that led from where they stood to the gap in his dad's hedge.

'What is it, Billy? It looks like something's been dragged.'

And there was another path of beaten-down grass, a straighter one this time, which led from the gap in the hawthorns to the nearest point of the Edge.

They followed it until they could look down over the cliff. But Billy could see nothing among the bramble-strewn boulders and small reeded ponds where they caught newts and tadpoles, not even a dead rabbit. But then he hadn't really expected to.

'What is it, Billy? What are you looking for?'

'It's just I think I know where that Ghost Dog is now.'

'Where?'

'Not a million miles from here,' he said, smiling.

'But how d'you know?'

'Elementary, my dear Ward,' he said.

If you believed the local bulletin after the evening news, he wasn't the only one.

The announcer told them that night that no less than three eye-witnesses had seen the Ghost Dog practically face to face that day.

It ranged in colour from pure white, through grey, to reddish-brown: the first eye-witness had seen it heading south out of Darlington. The second had observed it chasing sheep just west of Wolsingham. The third had been knocked off his bike by it on Newcastle Suspension bridge as he pedalled north. They'd all seen it within twenty minutes of one another.

'Must have a champion pair of legs on it, that dog!' Billy's dad jeered.

'Two pair, Dad,' said Billy.

'Well, one thing to be thankful for is it's not round here any more, eh, Dick?' said Billy's mam.

And as soon as she said that Billy said, 'Shall I see to the hens and pigeons tonight, then, Dad?'

'No,' his dad said. 'No, not just yet son. You don't want to believe everything you hear on the telly.'

And his mam said, 'Anybody fancy another cup of tea?' though they'd only just that minute had one. It was obvious she was trying to change the subject. 'I don't know what's the matter with me tonight,' she said, 'I'm just somehow parched!'

Billy nearly laughed his head off, but just on the quiet.

It was while his mam was forcing her second cup of tea that Elvis came round. He wanted Billy to come and see his dad's new videos.

'New videos?' asked Billy's dad. 'I thought your dad already had a newish video?'

'That one had to go back yesterday,' Elvis said.

'Didn't your dad fancy that one?' Billy's mam asked, fishing.

140

'He fancied it alright,' Elvis said, 'only we couldn't afford the payments. That's what for he's got these two new ones.'

'Why, how much are they costing him?' asked Billy's dad.

'Nowt. Me dad got them on a week's free trial. First he went into the shop and got one, then five minutes later he sent me mam in to sign for one.'

'I never knew that was allowed,' said Grandma.

'I don't think it is if you sign your own name,' said Elvis, 'but me dad always signs somebody else's.'

'Somebody else's!' said Billy's dad, nearly swallowing his pipe. 'Whose?'

'Sometimes he uses one name, sometimes another,' said Elvis. 'He spreads it around.'

'That's very nice of him, I'm sure,' said Billy's mam.

'And what in the world's your father want *two* videos for?' asked Billy's dad.

'So's he can mek twice as many copies,' said Elvis. 'He hires a video from the public library and meks twenty or thirty copies of it and then teks it back.'

'That *must* be illegal!' said Grandma.

'Me dad sez it isn't,' said Elvis, 'because we always give them back their video on time. He's mekkin' a canny profit at it,' he said smiling round at them proudly. 'The blank tapes he uses cost him practically nowt because they fell off the back of me Uncle Dasher's lorry, and me dad

141

sells them on Bishop Auckland market ten quid apiece. They go like hot cakes.'

'I bet they do!' said Billy's dad.

'That *must* be illegal,' said Billy's grandma.

'Only if they find out,' said Elvis.

Chapter 20

Elvis told him on the way round to their house what the rest of the Gang had got up to that afternoon.

When they got down to Doggy Wood, the Crag Enders were waiting for them and they nearly had a fight, but in the end signed a peace treaty and decided to go off and try and hunt down the Ghost Dog instead.

'Good idea,' Billy said, looking dead serious.

After that they'd met up with some fellars. They'd come from all over the shop: Middleham, Coxhoe — even two from Shilton. That would be the two that shot the squirrel, most probably, Billy thought. There were about thirty of them, six with guns, the rest with sticks. They'd walked for miles, Elvis said. Right through Doggy Woods, up to Sedgefield hospital, then across country to Gypsy Crossing and then back home. Every time they passed a pub, two or three of the men dropped out. By the time they got back to Crag End there were only three men left, and they were all smelling of beer and nine-parts legless.

'See any sign of the Ghost Dog?' Billy asked.

No, Elvis said, but they had shot a hen, accidentally, when it stirred in a hedge they were passing.

'Anyroad, it's up Newcastle way now by the

sound of it, else down Darlington way,' Billy said.

'I know. We saw it on the telly. Me da sez it must've split itself in three halves to confuse the bobbies!'

Elvis's dad was making his one hundred and ninety-second copy of a scary video when they went in the front room. Both videotapes were humming away like mad while he studied his *Racing Times*.

Elvis's sister was heating a needle over a last year's Christmas candle so she could stick a safety pin through her nose. It was the latest craze round their way. That, and going to the disco dressed in two bin-liners and black stockings that had holes in them.

She was sitting with her mam on a mattress on the floor: the sofa appeared to have gone back to the Co-op. Both ferrets were lolloping about the room chasing empty crisp packets.

'Come and sit down by me, pet,' said Mrs Potter, patting the six inches at her right side. 'And how's your mam?'

'Champion, Mrs Potter.'

'And how's your grandma? Was that her I saw getting off the bus?'

'She came down about twelve.'

'I thought it was her. She usually comes down *Sunday*, doesn't she, Billy?'

'Usually.'

'Mind, tell her I like her fur coat and moon boots, will you. They really suit her. Didn't I say so, Roger?'

'Aye,' said Mr Potter, without ceasing his studies.

'I expect she got them at the jumbly, did she?'

'I'm not sure,' said Billy.

'I expect so. You can get some real bargains at the jumblies nowadays. I got Mr Potter a lovely trench coat to go to the races in last week, didn't I?'

'Aye.'

'Only cost us twenty pence. Plenty of room in it and made of real canvas.'

'He looks like a tent in it!' said Soss.

'Shut your cheeky mouth!' said Mr Potter.

'Charming!'

'Want a chocolate, Billy? Where are me manners?' She lifted her bottom and extracted a battered box of Milk Tray which she offered to Billy.

Billy declined.

'They tell me your dad's factory's shuttin',' said Mr Potter. 'How's your dad reactin' to that?'

'I didn't know anything about it, Mr Potter.' That was actually true. 'He never tells me nothing.' So was that.

'It'll not suit your dad,' said Mr Potter. 'He's the sort that can't stand to exist without work.'

'Not like some we know!' said Soss.

'At least I've got more to do than stick holes in me nose!'

'You don't *stick* holes, Dad. You bore them!'

'You bore me, lass! I know where I'd like to stick that pin of yours, if I had half the chance.'

'It's not a pin, Dad. This is called a needle.'

'Pins! Needles! What's the difference?'

'You can't darn a stocking with a needle, can you, Mam?'

'Don't ask me,' said Mrs Potter, as she took a chocolate with a nut in it. She was very fond of nuts, as you might expect. 'I've never darned a stocking in me life!' That was true, and all. 'And how's things down in Barnsley, Billy? Sure you don't want a chocolate? I know they're a little bit melted.'

'No thanks, Mrs Potter. All right as far as I know.'

'Your Sandra's up, somebody was telling me, and the bairn?'

'They came on Friday.'

'And is Steven with them?'

'Not yet,' said Billy.

'Always a ladies' man, Steven,' said Mr Potter.

'At least he was a man!' said Soss.

'Shut your clatter! I've warned you! Sitting there like Bride of Dracula!'

'I'd marry anybody to get out of this house,' said Soss.

'And what for hasn't he come up, then, Billy?'

'Overtime,' said Billy. 'He's getting as much as he can in nowadays because Our Sandra wants a fitted kitchen.' All lies that. It had just come off the top of his head. 'Last week he did sixty hours.'

'Owwwers!' said Soss as the hot needle went through her nose. 'Owwers!'

147

'Serves you right,' said Mr Potter without looking up.

'I've just noticed something,' Mrs Potter said. 'You know that lad on the telly – he's the spitting image of you, Billy.'

'You mean that evil-looking one that pretends to be all innocent? Him that makes things happen?'

'You're exactly like him, Billy Robinson!'

Billy wasn't altogether surprised.

He wasn't altogether surprised, either, when Pinky wandered over and sunk her teeth into Mrs Potter's toe.

Chapter 21

Steven was standing in front of the fire warming his credentials when Billy got home. He looked white-faced, angry, and cold. Billy guessed he must have just driven up from Barnsley.

Billy's mother was sitting on the sofa, staring into space. His dad was sucking noisily on an empty pipe (had Grandma polished off all his baccy?) and looking like death warmed up, but only just.

The telly was off. Very definitely off.

After saying hello to Steven, Billy asked where Sandra and Julie were.

'Go and make yourself a cup of cocoa, Billy,' his mam said, 'then get yourself off to bed.'

'Can I just watch a bit of the match, Mam? Just a bit?'

She didn't answer.

He went into the kitchen, this time not bothering to shut the door behind him. Dot was lying in her basket under the kitchen table. She wasn't asleep. She had her golliwog tucked into her and was licking it. At least she seemed calmer now.

'Well, this is a fine kettle of fish,' he heard his dad say. He heard him knocking out his empty pipe on the bars of the fire-grate.

Billy put the kettle on and lit the gas.

'Do we know the lass?' he heard his mother ask.

There was a pause.

Billy reached down the cocoa and sugar. He took the milk from the fridge.

'It's no good standing there like a stuffed duck, Steven,' said Billy's dad, 'not if we're going to get to the bottom of this matter.'

'All I bliddy did was dance with a lass!' Steven exploded. 'That's the top and bottom of the matter.'

'Well, I don't know,' said Billy's mother. 'There must have been more to it than that.'

'Well, I'm telling you there wasn't!'

'And who was she?' asked Billy's dad.

'Tommy Blamire's daughter. Her and her husband's just moved down here.'

'Isn't she the one that was Miss Northern Coal a few years back?' asked Billy's mam. 'Didn't she once pose for a photo in one of them magazines?'

'She might've done,' said Steven. 'I can't remember.'

'Well, you want your head examining, that's all I can say,' said Billy's dad. 'Common sense should've told you what Our Sandra would feel looking on at that palaver. She's always been a bit on the jealous side.'

'A bit! A bit!' said Steven. Then he said something else. A swear word. It was the second-worst swear word Billy knew. He said it that loud all the water pipes started ringing. The whole street must have heard it. Certainly

150

the Murrays next door must have heard it, and they were watching a motorbike rally on the telly at full blast. And there was no doubt at all that Sandra and Julie must have heard it upstairs in the bedroom, if that was where they were living.

'Well, in all my life I've never heard language like that in this house,' said Billy's mam.

Steven said it again. The same word. Even louder. Maybe even the motorbike riders heard it this time.

'I fail to see what good shouting's going to do,' said Billy's dad. 'Shouting never mended a matter.'

'Nor did swearing, neither,' said Billy's mam.

'Mebbies her up there'll hear it!' shouted Steven.

'I doubt very much if it'll impress her,' said Billy's dad.

'I'd like to fly up them stairs and grab hold of her this minute!' said Steven. 'That's what I'd like to do.'

'You'll not, Steven. Because if you try, *I'll* stop you.'

Billy's dad wasn't as big as Steven, but he could be terribly awkward when he wanted to.

'I'll tell you one thing – I'm not going back without her!'

'Nobody wants you to.'

'When I leave this house, she comes with me. Her and that bairn. Whether she wants to or not!'

151

'I doubt you'll have a job on your hands, Steven.'

'Who says?'

'Our Sandra'll say. You know what she's like. She's always had a will of her own. You knew that when you married her. You should've thought of it before.'

'It was you that was at fault in the first place, Steven,' said Billy's mam.

'Nobody's arguing the toss over that!'

'Keep your hair on, Steven,' said Billy's dad.

'I am keeping it on!' shouted Steven.

The water pipes started tuning up again.

Billy made his cocoa. Things weren't getting any better. If anything they were going from bad to worse. He took his cocoa into the other room.

'Can I just watch a bit of that match, Mam? It's Sunderland tonight.'

'Straight up those stairs, young man,' she said.

'Sunderland?' said his dad. 'Is Sunderland on tonight? I thought that match was off.'

'It's on again now, Dad. They said on the news.'

'Up!' said Billy's mam, jerking her thumb bedroomwards.

'Let the lad finish his cocoa in the warm, Alice,' said his dad. 'What time's the match start, son?'

Billy was just going to say 'One minute' when the passage door flew open and his sister went flying through the room at about ninety miles an hour, her eyes fixed blankly ahead and apparently seeing nothing. She went into the kitchen for something, then came back out again and went past them looking to neither left nor right, and was gone.

'You can see the state the lass's in,' said Billy's dad.

'I don't give twopence what state she's in!' shouted Steven, aiming his abuse at the closed passage door. 'When I leave this house, *she* comes with me – her and that bairn!'

'Maybe it *would* be a good idea to have the football on,' said Billy's mam.

There was a pause. Then both men spoke together. They both said the same words:

'It makes no odds to me.'

They looked at one another for a second or two. Then they both burst out laughing.

'I've heard that great minds think alike,' said Billy's dad, 'but this is the first time I've seen it proved!'

'That must be it, man!'

'I'll make a pot of tea,' said Billy's mam, standing up, 'I don't want to watch this tripe.'

'It's not tripe, Mam,' said Billy. 'I told you it was Sunderland.'

'*And* it's a Cup match!' said Steven.

'I'd rather have a cup of tea,' she said. 'You might as well sit yourself down, Steven, you'll only wear the mat out if you stand there all night.'

Steven sat on the sofa next to Billy who had switched on the telly with the sound low. The motorbikes were still buzzing.

'Playing for the school team yet, son?' asked Steven.

'I had my first game last Saturday.'

'Thought you'd have been captain by now!'

'He's over-young yet,' said Billy's dad. 'There was some lads in the teams thirteen — but he didn't play bad.'

'I was the youngest ever to play for the school team,' said Billy trying to look modest.

'Who'd you play?'

'Middleham Middle,' said Billy.

'All their team's only got one leg, haven't they?'

'You'd have thought so by the score,' said Billy, 'we won 7–1.'

'And Our Billy's scored the third goal, didn't you son?' said Billy's dad, not making the slightest effort to look modest at all.

'Pity he'll never be as good as me,' said Steven. 'When I played for the Athletic they used to call me the Georgie Best of Belton Buildings!'

'I never knew you were always getting chucked out of nightclubs!' said Billy.

Steven gave him a welter on the arm, so Billy punched him in the ribs and they started a wrestling match.

'You two are not fighting on my best sofa?' shouted Billy's mam from the kitchen.

'I never knew we had another one, Mam,' said Billy, looking round.

'Give over, the pair of you,' said Billy's dad.

'Turn that telly up, Billy. Not over much.'

The motorbikes had buzzed off now, and the programme presenter was talking to himself till Billy adjusted the volume.

'. . . and tonight, for those of our viewers who feel goal-starved by our recent match coverage, we have something of a treat in store. Sheffield Wednesday were at home to Sunderland this afternoon, and as you might expect from these two excellent teams, both fighting for promotion at the top of Division Two, this was a game full of verve, enterprise – and I'm sure something we'd *all* like to see on this programme: goals.'

'Pity Sunderland didn't score enough, though,' said Steven.

'Lose, did they?' asked Billy's dad. 'I didn't catch the scores.'

'Four-three,' said Billy. 'It was one all at half-time.'

'What a pity,' said Billy's dad. 'Mebbies we all play best at home.'

'Aye,' said Steven thoughtfully, 'I think that's true enough.'

It was shortly after that Billy's dad brought a couple of beers in from the fridge. He was just opening them and handing one to Steven, when Sandra banged through the passage door and did her flying-blind-through-the-room act again and went into the kitchen.

When she came back, though, she paused long enough to howl down the back of Steven's neck:

'Is that all you can do at a time like this? Watch football and drink beer?'

Then she was gone.

'That's a definite improvement,' said Billy's dad, lighting up a cigar. 'At least she's talking to you now, Steven. I take it you'll be sleeping here tonight? You don't mind kipping on the sofa?'

Chapter 22

Billy's dad was right about things improving because next morning Sandra threw the Cornflakes packet at Steven's head when they were having breakfast.

'Contact!' shouted Billy's dad. 'That's more like it now, lass. Why don't you throw the sugarbowl at him, and all?'

Sandra didn't feel quite up to an act of that generosity, so she threw the cosy from the teapot at Steven instead. Then she rushed out of the kitchen at the speed of light.

'That's what we want to see!' laughed Billy's dad.

'I can't see what you've got to be so cheerful about,' Billy's mam said.

'You have to look on the bright side, Alice. She could easy have chucked the teapot at him!'

Grandma arrived after church – just as Billy's mam was peeling the spuds for dinner. Mr Wainwright, who had been Grandad's marrer down the pit, fetched her down in his ancient Anglia that Steven always said they wouldn't allow in a veteran car rally in case it died in the attempt. Mr Wainwright was a little scraggy feller – he was always kidding Billy on that you had to be little to get through the coalseams in his day – and when he drove his car, he was that

157

low down in the seat you could hardly see him. It looked like the car was driving itself.

Grandma wasn't wearing her moon boots and fur coat this time. She had her black coat on, a pair of white gloves, and a smart pair of black shoes.

'My feet's killing me,' she said as she came through the back door. 'I've been praying for mercy all through the service. I thought the Vicar was never going to stop.'

'What for didn't you take them off in the car, Mother?'

'I kept telling her to,' said Mr Wainwright.

'I'd never have got them on again,' said Grandma. 'I would've looked a fool walking up the street in me stockinged feet!'

'You'll die of vanity one of these days, Mother.'

'Well, I intend to look smart when I go, Alice,' said Grandma. 'I'm not going looking slovenly, not in front of Our Lord.' She sat down at the table and, with a struggle, prised off her shoes. 'Thanks be to God for small mercies!' Then she looked at little Julie. 'Hello, pet. Are you drinking your milk?'

'D'inkin' milk G'andma,' said Julie, sticking her nose back in the cup.

'And have you come to your senses now, young man?' Grandma asked, looking at Steven.

'As far as is humanly possible in a man of my mental ability,' said Steven, smiling at her.

'The cold war's near enough over, Mother,'

said Billy's dad, 'so they won't want you laying down the law and starting it all over again.'

'I'm sorry I spoke,' said Grandma in a huff. 'There's not a drop of tea in that pot, Alice?'

But things got better after all that. They all sat in the other room and admired little Julie, and said how big she'd grown and how forward for her age she was and how well-behaved she was compared to other children nowadays.

Steven and Sandra sat on the sofa, at different ends of it, with Grandma in the middle like a referee, and Billy's mam and dad perched on the outside arms like a pair of linesmen.

After exhausting the possibilities of little Julie as a discussion point, they switched to other matters of interest: how cold it had been; how Mr Wainwright's cat had fleas again; how the Co-op had put up the price of its cornplasters by ten pence in the last six months; how Mrs Drury's husband had hit three bum notes on the organ in one single verse of *Rock of Ages*, making Grandma wonder, yet again, if he was up to something he shouldn't be. She was always spreading rumours about the Drurys and she seemed to be convinced that Mr Drury was having a carry-on with another woman in the congregation: but with Grandma it was always possible she was lying her head off.

After dinner Steven and Sandra dried the cutlery together. They still didn't speak, not to one another, but Sandra did pass behind him several times without once actually stabbing him in the back.

159

After coffee and mints – Mr Wainwright had given Grandma a box of After Eights – little Julie fell asleep on the sofa and Steven was allowed to pop her upstairs to bed. When he came back down again Grandma said, as if she'd just thought of it:

'Why don't you two take yourselves out for a walk while that bairn's asleep?'

'A breath of fresh air'll do you both good,' said Billy's mam.

'Get yourselves along to Foxcover,' said his dad, 'before they chop it down.'

Steven looked at Sandra. At first she didn't want to. But then she changed her mind.

It was nearly half past two when they came back and by then they were *nearly* holding hands. Sandra put some lipstick on in the kitchen and Steven went upstairs to get Julie up.

After that they sat on the sofa, together this time though not actually touching, and passed little Julie back and forth between them as if she were a beach ball. Gradually her thumb came out of her mouth.

When Billy said, 'Where's that cheeky girl? I'm going to eat her toes off!' she ran giggling into the kitchen and hid under the table while Billy shambled towards her on his hands and knees pretending to be a mad dog. 'No! No! No!' she kept shouting. She really loved that game. Especially pulling his hair and trying to separate his ears from the rest of his head.

Afterwards Billy liked to think it was maybe

this bit of excitement and noise that finally did the trick with Steven and his sister, because certainly when he went back into the room things had changed.

First Steven was saying it was all his fault, then Sandra said no, *she* was the one to blame, then Steven said he was sorry and Sandra said he had no right to be because it was *her* that should be sorry.

They managed to stretch it out quite a long time.

'You know I love you,' said Steven, who could be terribly soppy at times.

She took his hand and squeezed it. 'It was all my silly fault.'

They leaned together slowly. Oh no! thought Billy. He knew exactly what was going to happen. Eventually they kissed above Julie's head, who had bobbed back in between them. It was quite embarrassing.

Grandma, who had appeared to be nodding off, jumped to her feet and clapped her hands together. 'Kiss and make up! That's it – kiss and make up!' She hobbled over and embraced them both in turn, nearly falling on them. All three were crying. 'And that little bairn!' said Grandma, bending down to kiss Julie. Then she hobbled back to the chair and collapsed in it.

'Thank the Lord for that,' said Billy's dad.

'Kiss and make up,' said Grandma, 'that's all that matters. Never mind whose fault it was. That's all in the past now.' She dabbed her eyes with her hanky and wiped a drop off the end of her nose. 'I *am* pleased. I only wish your grandad had been here to see this day. He wouldn't have missed it for anything, if he hadn't gone and died first.'

'It's a blessing, I'm sure,' said Billy's mam. Tears were streaming down her cheeks like a minor flood disaster.

'It is a blessing, Our Alice,' said Grandma, 'and God works in a mysterious way. I've told you that before, but nobody ever takes any notice of me.' She dabbed and sniffed a couple of times, and then said, 'All I know is I asked God to do something about this business this morning in Church, and if this isn't proof that he listens to me, well, I'll eat the next door's cat!'

Chapter 23

It was after Sunday tea that Billy's dad told him he knew where the Ghost Dog was. 'I've known for a canny bit and all, Billy,' he said. 'Ever since Wednesday morning.'

He leaned back, reached for his pipe, and lit it up. He looked ever so smug. Absolutely chuffed with himself.

'Where is it, Dad?' Billy asked, trying to look all innocent.

'Up in the allotment, Billy. In the pigeon hut.'

Now Billy stopped looking innocent and switched to looking surprised instead.

'Blinking heck, Dad!' said Billy.

'Stop using language, Our Billy!' shouted his mam from the kitchen where she was washing-up with Sandra. 'We don't want no swearing in this house!'

'I can see that's taken the wind out of your sails!' his dad said, leaning back even further and puffing out more smoke.

'I'm flabbergasted, Dad,' said Billy, acting the part really well.

His dad laughed appreciatively.

Last year Miss Benfold's class had done a pantomime for the whole school called Ali Boo Boo and the Magic Vacuum-cleaner of Baghdad, and Billy had played the part of the evil genie called Abu Ben Uglymug. Everybody had said

163

how brilliant he had been: his mam, Sandra, Grandma, and the woman next door. Even Steven had said he was just right for the part.

'Would you like to come up and see her after it's got dark?' his dad asked. 'Give her a bit of a stroke?'

It was now time for Billy to switch from looking surprised to looking shocked, petrified and scared. In the last act of the pantomime he'd had to look shocked, petrified and scared when an even uglier and more evil genie hired by the prince had been sent to frighten him away from the palace. Mind you, in the pantomime it had been easy to look shocked, petrified and scared because the part of the uglier and more evil genie had been played by Elvis.

'I found her when I went up to get the eggs you'd left up at the allotment,' his dad said. 'It was Dot that led me to her. She knew what was going on all right!' Billy smiled to himself when he remembered how many times his dad called Dot an idiot, but he said nothing. 'And I don't mind admitting I was a bit scared when I first clapped eyes on the beast, Billy. She *was* a size, and no mistake.' He puffed smoke. 'But there was no harm in her, no harm at all. You could see that in a trice. She'd just been badly used, that's all.'

'What did you do, Dad?'

'Some daft nitwit that wants stringing up by his toenails had let fly at her with his shotgun. She was nine-parts dead already. Not only that, she'd had three pups while she was up there.

164

Two of them had died. That was the pong you mentioned. But the other one is still surviving – just.'

Billy's mother came in, undoing her pinny.

'Then we cleaned her up, didn't we Dick?'

'Aye. Your mother came up and helped. I couldn't have managed on me own. We washed her with TCP.'

'Fancy that!' said Billy.

'Your mother managed to get most of the bits of shot out of her wounds, like.'

'And she never so much as showed her teeth, did she, Dick?'

'Not once. Then we dragged her on a tarpaulin all the way back to the allotment. There was no chance of lifting her, like, she was too poorly for that.'

'What for didn't you tell us, Dad?'

'That was my fault, Billy,' said his mam. 'I told your dad not to because—'

'We *were* going to tell you that night you got back late. Only, when you'd waited for that Potter lad we got the wind up.'

'You don't know what the Potters are like, Billy,' his mam said. 'They'll wangle anything out of anybody. You have to be that careful.'

'That's why I laid a false trail,' his dad said. 'We put a sack of taties on the same tarpaulin and dragged it to the Edge. In case Dasher Potter and his terriers got up there. Put them off the scent, like. Mek it look like the dog had gone over the cliff.'

'What a brilliant idea! Nobody'd ever think of

that!' said Billy, giving a brilliant performance as he uttered the lines.

And his dad puffed so much smoke that for a moment he was lost from view behind enormous clouds of self-appreciation.

An hour later, when it was properly dark, they went up to the allotment: Billy, his dad, and Steven – and Dot, of course. They couldn't have left her behind if they'd tried.

Billy carried a plastic bag full of his mam's home-made dog meat, Steven a bucket of water, and Billy's dad had his torch – not switched on in case anyone saw – and the old towel they used to dry Dot with after one of her reluctant baths. Dot herself, obviously feeling dead important, led the way up the twisting path ahead of them, the white tip of her tail constantly disappearing round the next bend.

They walked in silence. Billy's dad didn't even smoke his pipe. They must have picked an ideal time, because from shutting the backyard gate behind them to opening the door of the pigeon hut they didn't see a single soul.

The Ghost Dog was lying full-length on some newspapers and old sacking when they went into the pigeon hut. She practically stretched the whole width of the floor. Never in all his dreams had Billy ever imagined such a big dog could exist.

Her hair was grey and thick. It was matted with mud and thorns. Her eyes were soft and tired-looking. A single pup was suckling from her.

She lifted her head when they entered, and gave a long, low growl; but when Billy's dad spoke to her quietly she allowed her massive head to sink back again into rest.

Before they were all properly in the hut, Dot had stepped daintily between the outstretched legs of the Ghost Dog and seated herself as close to the pup as she could. When the pup interrupted its suckling to squeak, her ears twitched and she bent down and licked it. The Ghost Dog lifted her head just to make sure everything was all right, then sank back again with a sigh.

Billy's dad fastened the door shut, then placed the torch on the floor where it would throw less light.

'My God, but she's in a state!' said Steven.

'She's had a hard time of it, Steven, and no mistake.'

'What sort of dog is she, Dad?' asked Billy.

'It's my guess she's an Irish Wolfhound. But I couldn't swear to it.'

He moved down the hut.

'Come out of the way, lass,' he said to Dot.

She had to be edged aside, and even then kept wriggling her bottom back to where it had come from.

Billy's dad knelt by the Ghost Dog and began to stroke her gently:

'There, there, now. All right now, lass.'

He filled her waterbowl and put some dog meat in another. The Ghost Dog lifted her head and forequarters, and started to drink. The pup rolled off her and began to squeak its annoyance. Dot's ears twitched up and down with concern. She even tried to nose the pup back onto its teat. Billy's dad did the job for her.

'What did you do with the other pups, Dad?'

'Buried them under the lilac bush, Billy.'

The Ghost Dog had finished drinking now. She didn't seem interested in the food. She lay down again. Billy's dad was already washing off the mud and picking out the thorns.

'I've already got a lot of pellets out of her,' he said, 'but there's still a bonny lot left in. She'll have to go to a vet's if you *do* take her back down Barnsley with you, Steven. What do you think!'

'I'm game,' said Steven.

'Good lad. And what's Our Sandra say?'

'You know what your Sandra's like – she wouldn't dream of leaving it behind.'

'I thought she wouldn't.'

He was drying off the Ghost Dog now. She seemed to be almost sleeping. Dot had somehow manoeuvred herself back in so that her own belly was actually touching the pup.

'If she stays here much longer she'll be a dead 'un,' said Billy's dad. 'And that would be a shame. There's not an ounce of harm in her. If there was, she'd have had my pigeons by now. But the fact is she's as gentle as a lamb. The rest is just fears and rumours.'

For the first time Billy was aware of the pigeons shuffling above his head. They must have had a pretty anxious time of it for the last three days, he thought.

169

'What will you do with her, Steven? Will you keep her for yourselves?' asked Billy's dad.

'I doubt it, Dick. We'll put an advert in the paper once she's up on her pins. Things are a bit unsettled down there, like. There's talk of the pit shutting down where I am.'

'It's the same over the whole country, Steven. There's a rumour going round about the factory now, they might be shutting that. I just can't understand it at all. The whole country's going down the drain.' He stood up. 'We'll leave the food for her. She'll mebbies touch it when she's hungry. What time shall we come up for her then? We better make an early start.'

'Five o'clock all right?' asked Steven.

Chapter 24

Billy was awake long before five the next morning. He heard the birds start singing on the gutters and in the bushes up in the allotments when it was still pitch dark – or pitch dark to anybody but the birds.

It was called the Dawn Chorus. His grandma had told him that. It was when the first crack of light appeared over the horizon and all the birds started tuning up for another day.

His grandma made out she was always hearing it nowadays, because it was the time when Grandad was due to get out of bed and report back to Heaven again, but Billy reckoned she had her wires a bit twisted there and got him mixed up with a vampire: she'd probably been watching too many Dracula movies.

Just before the downstairs clock chimed five, he heard a bump that might have been the back door closing: he guessed it would be his dad and Steven going up for the Ghost Dog.

It was freezing in his room when he got out of bed. It was no wonder Count Dracula went haring back to his coffin when the dawn came. Anybody in their right senses would. He pulled his jersey on over his pyjamas and then put his dressing gown on, and his woolly Sunderland supporters hat that his grandma had got him from an Oxfam shop.

Downstairs, somebody had already lit the fire. And Julie had been brought down wrapped in her blankets, and laid on the sofa still fast asleep. It was funny the way she'd slept practically the whole time she'd been here. Either that or just stared into the fire with her thumb in her mouth.

Maybe it was the best thing to do. Maybe that was how people got themselves through a hard time? Just slept through it. Like animals going into suspended animation so they could endure the cold hand of winter.

His mam and sister were in the kitchen, standing by the gas fire with all its burners lit and warming up their noses over cups of steaming tea.

His mam poured him a cup as he came in.

'Thought you were never going to join the land of the living!' she joked. She looked cold and drawn, but that was the first time she'd really laughed for days. She handed him his tea. 'Never known him be this eager for school on a Monday morning, Our Sandra!'

Sandra smiled at Billy. 'Not like Our Billy at all,' she said.

Billy smiled back. He didn't say anything, he felt it was too early for talking just yet. He felt like one of the zombies in one of Mr Potter's videos, a bit slow-moving, as if his blood hadn't thawed out properly just yet. And it was a sight too soon to be blinking Monday morning as well. Another week of work and trouble looming up ahead. It wasn't fair!

'What do you think you'll do then?' Billy's mam asked Sandra, resuming a conversation they must have been having before.

'We don't know yet, Mam. Steven says if he gets made redundant down there he'll have had enough.'

'You mean you'll shift back up here again?'

'That's what he thinks. I mean, it's not that we don't get on with folks down there.'

'No.'

'It's just that if they closed the pit where he is now, he thinks we may as well move back up here, where we belong, like.'

Billy's mam didn't say anything, but Billy knew what she was thinking. There was no work to be had up here. People were shifting out of Belton, not moving back into it. There were three houses for sale down Bertha Street alone. And if the factory really did close . . .

They heard the front door open and shut quietly, and a minute later Billy's dad came into the kitchen, rubbing his hands together.

'By God, but she's parky out there!'

'How did you manage with the dog?' Billy's mam asked.

'Not a bit of bother. She seemed to understand what was going on. Only trouble was getting her down to the car. Good job that husband of yours has got a bit of muscle, Sandra. She still isn't in a fit state to move herself.'

'Did she eat her food up?'

'Finished the lot, Alice. Might as well wrap the rest up and give them it to take down to Barnsley.'

173

'Is the pup all right, Dad?'

'Right as rain, son. Fat as butter. You can see the difference in it already.'

Steven came in and looked at Sandra.

'Are you right, lass? I've put the bairn in the car already.'

'What'll you do, Steven?' asked Billy's dad. 'Just let the car roll down the fronts on her own steam?'

Steven nodded. 'With a bit of luck we won't need to use the engine till we get down to Station Road. After that we'll be on the motorway in fifteen minutes.'

'If I'm not mistaken,' said Billy's dad, 'that'll be where she's come from in the first place. Some wicked devils'll have got tired of her and just dumped her.'

'Folks like that want shooting,' said Sandra.

'You just can't understand their mentality,' said Billy's mam.

'It's a funny world we live in nowadays,' said Billy's dad.

'We'd better be off, Mam,' said Sandra. 'Ta-ra. Ta-ra, Dad. Ta-ra, Our Billy.' She kissed them all. 'And thanks a lot for all you've done.'

'Aye, thanks a lot,' said Steven.

'Don't thank us,' said Billy's dad. 'You owe us nowt. It's us that owes you for tekkin' that dog off our hands. We could've easy got run in by the Police over that.'

They all trooped out into the street to see the Ghost Dog and her pup. They didn't speak a

word. The car doors were clunked shut as quietly as possible.

Looking in at the back of the Cortina through the steamed-up windows reminded Billy of looking into the aquarium in Mrs Drury's classroom. He lifted up Dot so she could see. The pup was sprawled on Dot's old blanket, its eyes tight shut: like Julie, it seemed to be sleeping through it all.

The Ghost Dog was sitting up now, her head scraping the inside lining of the roof. She was cramped but happy-looking. Her tongue was lolling out. Her breath had almost obscured the glass of the back window as Steven let go the handbrake and the car began to slide slowly and silently down the fronts.

A moment later the Ghost Dog had vanished back into the mists where she'd first come from: and that was the last Billy ever saw of her.